F

In early December I of
a large bushfire burning d
thought, that's unusually season. I
shrugged and got on with life. You see, I live in Perth,
Western Australia, some 5000 kilometres or more away
from that fire burning near the East Coast. I noted that
some blamed global warming, and some blamed the
proponents of global warming in forcing the
governments to cut back on burning off programs in
winter to reduce the amount of carbon being put in the
atmosphere. Again, I shrugged and got on with life.

Since then the number and intensity of the fires have
spread exponentially, and as I write this, every single
state in Australia is suffering major fires, many
hopelessly out of control. Estimates of how many and
how big vary, but one source says as of today 17.9
million acres of Australia have burned in one of the
country's worst fire seasons on record. That's an area
larger than West Virginia, and more than eight times the
area that burned in California in 2018—and the fires are
still burning out of control.

I find, when people talk really big numbers I switch
off, because they are too big to contemplate, however,
another report says that well over one billion native
animals and birds have lost their lives…one billion.

Like most Australians I wanted to do something
about it. But what could I do other than give money,
which I have done. The problem is that it's nowhere near
enough; a tiny drop in the ocean of what is needed. Then
I had an idea.

I am very fortunate as a writer to have a wonderful

publisher in the US, The Wild Rose Press, and a part of the benefit is that I belong to an author group under the auspices of TWRP. We have a forum loop, where we assist each other in all sorts of areas; it is a wonderful feeling of comradeship as everyone experiences the same issues, frustrations, and joys. I sent an email to the loop asking if there was any interest in authors donating a short story and foregoing any royalties so that all proceeds could be donated to the bushfire appeal if there was enough for an anthology. I thought if I could generate some interest, hopefully I could ask TWRP to publish it, but that if it did not seem feasible from a logistical point of view, I would seek help and self-publish it, because as an author, what better way is there for me to help those who have lost everything, than to write?

Well, the response was phenomenal and over the weekend that followed I received over four hundred emails pledging stories, support, editorial help and a narrator to perform an audio version. Best of all, the President of TWRP, Rhonda Penders, emailed me, even though she was away, expressing her enthusiasm and willingness to support such an anthology.

I started out by hoping I could coax a dozen or so authors to give me a story they would lose the rights to, yet by Sunday night I had forty-four of them! And all of those who didn't or couldn't have a story ready for the deadline, without exception, wanted to help in whatever way they could. Most (but not all) live in the US and news had travelled to them just how bad the fires are, and everyone's generosity was wonderful. In fact, I had so many offers to help edit, format, cover design, narrate, even a self-publishing route was doable. Then Rhonda emailed again just before I was to crash into bed exhausted, to say she had spoken with her partner, RJ, and they wanted to take over the publishing. My dream suddenly became reality and this book you are reading took wings.

I have so many people to thank, I can't even begin to for fear I will miss some, but you all know who you are and I, and all the people of Australia thank you for your generosity of time and spirit to make this happen.

Also, thank you dear reader for buying this anthology, and supporting the victims of the worst fire ever. I sincerely hope you enjoy some of the best authors I know as they each present a tale they chose to donate. Some of these stories took a long time to write, edit, re-write, and edit a whole lot more, yet each was willing to give it to you.

Please enjoy, and sincerely, thank you.

Stephen B King
Perth, Western Australia
13th January 2020

Australia Burns

Volume 1

A collection of Fiction Short Stories

Mainstream
Women's Fiction
Thriller
Mystery

This is a work of fiction. Names, characters, places, and incidents are either the product of the author's imagination or are used fictitiously, and any resemblance to actual persons living or dead, business establishments, events, or locales, is entirely coincidental.

All proceeds from this publication will be donated to one or more organizations assisting in the fire relief effort in Australia.

Australia Burns, Volume One

The Wild Rose Press, Inc.
PO Box 708
Adams Basin, NY 14410-0708
Visit us at www.thewildrosepress.com

Publishing History
First Edition, 2020
Print ISBN 978-1-5092-3102-7
Digital ISBN 978-1-5092-3103-4

Published in the United States of America

Table of Contents

A Solicitous Wife

by

Madeleine McDonald

*First published in the Dreaming of Steam anthology
by Fantastic Books Publishing, 2017*

"I say, your skirt's rather short, isn't it?"

Elizabeth repressed a sigh. If only Mama had explained how difficult life with a husband would be. "Shorter skirts are practical, Richard. We are taking the train today, and I find it far easier to climb in and out of the carriage dressed like this." She demonstrated by lifting the skirt free of her ankles and lifting each knee in turn.

A month earlier, as a bride, she would have pirouetted in her new outfit for Richard's approval. In that month she had learned to suppress spontaneity.

"As you wish," he said. "But my mother never complained." In the doorway he turned back. His gaze was fond. "You always look charming to me. But I have a reputation to consider, and it would not do for people to say my wife looks fast."

"No, dearest."

Before her marriage, Elizabeth had taken her problems to Frances. War committee work took up all Mama's time, and her younger sister's new governess treated her like a grown-up. However, Frances was unmarried; it was impossible to ask her advice now.

Richard's proposal had come as a surprise, for he was a business acquaintance of her father. Papa pointed out the advantages of the match, when peace had brought further upheaval and so many young men had not come home from the trenches. Elizabeth knew she could not afford to be choosy. Richard might be a generation older, but he was established in his profession and offered financial security. Also, he seemed a kind man.

Running upstairs to find a hat, Elizabeth reflected that Richard might have a point. A solicitor's wife was always in the public eye, and he was well-known in Malton. She hesitated between last year's cloche and the latest sporty beret style. The day did promise to be warm, but would Richard call a beret fast, especially one embroidered in red? He was unpredictable. She chose the cloche and found a loose cardigan to go over her navy skirt, rather than the matching coat the seamstress had delivered.

By the time they walked to the station, any discontent had evaporated. She loved their trips to Malton market and never tired of the views from the train windows. City bred and accustomed to the grime of Leeds, she found the open, rolling country of the Yorkshire Wolds a revelation. The villages lay hidden in hollows, protected from winter's blasts. From the train, the seemingly bare landscape lacked the dark grandeur of the Pennines but entranced her all the more for that. Trees were rare, and try as she might, she could see no corner that had not been tilled or cultivated. The huge, sloping fields were already golden with corn, and in some, the reapers had begun work, walking behind the binder to stack the sheaves into stooks. Elizabeth tugged at Richard's sleeve whenever she saw it was a tractor that pulled the binder.

"Look, there's another one." The snub-nosed tractors, with their small front wheels and huge back ones, fascinated her. She had once been taken out in a motor car and found the ride thrilling.

Richard rustled his newspaper. "Progress, some

would say. I'm sorry to see the horses go, myself, but the farmers tell me one machine does the same work as a team of horses. What with the price of wheat falling, they have no choice."

Elizabeth went back to staring out of the window.

****

Two passengers alighted, leaving them alone in their first-class carriage.

Richard put down his newspaper and coughed. "As you know, I consulted Dr. Carroll yesterday. He suggested I keep a record of my irregularity. I shall rely on you to keep the record up to date, and to coordinate it with your choice of menus."

Elizabeth stared. What was this new wifely duty? Mama had informed her about a husband's expectations, and truth to tell, Elizabeth found the intimate side of marriage more enjoyable than she anticipated. It also put Richard in a good mood, which was another excellent reason to encourage his attentions.

"What do you mean, dearest?"

His tone was brisk. "I went this morning, for the first time in four days. You may start with that."

"Oh, you mean…you mean…"

"A call of nature, yes, Elizabeth. As my wife, you will take a close interest in my health. Carroll says bodily hygiene is most important for a man. Irregularity can be injurious to health as well as uncomfortable."

Elizabeth retrieved her diary from her capacious handbag. It seemed the most appropriate place to record the startling information. The train jolted, and her pencil streaked across the page. "Four days, yes, it is noted. Should I also write down what medicines you are taking?"

"Senna, liquorice, and—" He broke off. "What on earth are those squiggles?"

"Shorthand. I don't know how well I will read it back; the train is jolting me so. But I will remember." Pride in her accomplishments loosened her tongue. Richard must surely approve of a clever wife. "In case one of the servants should happen to find my diary, dearest. I know you would prefer such details to be kept private, as a matter between you and me." She showed him the page. "See. My sister's governess taught me shorthand. It is a most intriguing system. Does your clerk write shorthand? I understand it to be useful in business."

"Certainly not. He writes an excellent copperplate hand."

"Frances, our governess, learned it because she thought women might need to earn their own money after the war. And that is true. I hear there are now young ladies who take employment as typewriters."

Richard frowned. "But they are not from families such as yours. Do your parents know she holds such views? Surely she is not one of those tiresome suffragettes?"

"Of course not," Elizabeth lied, reflecting that votes for women was another subject of conversation to avoid in the future. Marriage was indeed a minefield. She distracted Richard by stroking his hand. In private, he showed a remarkable readiness to respond to her advances, and it was a most useful way of changing the subject. "Remember, dearest, it is my destiny to be interested in the modern world. I was born in the new century."

Richard stroked her hand in turn. "Twenty in 1920, how could I ever forget? An old man like me is lucky to have you."

Late in the afternoon, when they returned home, Elizabeth stole a nasturtium flower from the station display. In the privacy of her bedroom, she tucked the flower into her diary as a marker. Her fingers caressed the embossed cover as she put it away.

Her innermost thoughts would be safe. In shorthand, her diary would be as impenetrable to her husband as if written in Ancient Greek. He would be content to know that she was keeping a daily record of his health, as a good wife should.

.

No One Knew

by

Larry Farmer

She was too shy to speak, even if she had known English. He was everything. Just like the heroes on the Disney shows she glimpsed sometimes when her mother cleaned the house of *el Patrón*, their lord-like employer who owned the vast estate her entire family lived on and served as laborers in the fields and household.

Even at six, she sensed she had no place in his life. The dreams, at least, seemed real to her.

His hair was bright like the sun, while his eyes sparkled blue as the sky. His skin was white like the cotton that made money for *el Patrón* on the farm. In summers, his skin turned golden as he helped his father drive the machines in the fields. Her father drove them sometimes too, but his father owned them. And the fields.

He was so much older than her. Old enough to play what the Texans called football for the high school nearby. She was not surprised when her mother showed his picture in the newspaper from their town. The writing under these pictures, they both guessed, must talk of his wonders.

"The son of *el Patrón*," her mother said in Spanish, "has the grace of a deer. *El Patrón* named him David, like the king in the Bible. Everyone shows him respect as if he was a soldier in the war across the oceans. Can you imagine? As if he was a soldier in the war. We are honored to work for this *Patrón* and his son. It makes us special, Rosalinda."

She eventually learned English in the little school near the farm, though she did not speak it well. Her accent made her even more shy. But she kept a journal. Mostly about him, David, son of *el Patrón*.

And no one knew of her love for him, but God.

He is in the war now, she wrote one day. *Let him come home safely, sweet Jesus. Did he ever notice me when I was with Mamá? Does he ever think of me in this faraway land? I can only hope such a thing. But my skin and eyes and hair are dark like the dirt my mother sweeps. But his heart must be good. Surely, he must think of me sometimes. This girl that served his family in his home. And didn't Jesus say, blessed are the meek?*

"David has won a medal," her mother said with joy one day. "*El Patrón* tells everyone. Even the newspaper wrote about him, this time as a hero in the war."

She was eleven when he came back from the army. But then he went away again to college.

"He must be smart, this David," her mother said. "He will make a good *Patrón* someday that we will gladly serve."

I saw him, she wrote in her journal. *He is home for the summer to help his father on the farm, and he came into the house while I was there with Mamá cleaning. I speak English well, but my accent is still so strong and I was too shy again to speak to him. I use too much Spanish with my parents and my friends. How can I make my English better with so much Spanish? David is not just the son of* el Patrón, *he is educated. Maybe he looks down on me for the way I pronounce my words.*

Everyone said she was pretty now that she nearly a woman. Fifteen years old was nearly a woman to some. And now he was home for good helping his father.

"He is twenty-five and still not married, Rosalinda," her mother said with a sigh. "I heard last spring that the girl he was to marry did not want to live on a farm, and now they hate each other. What nonsense. These white people are as crazy as we are. But we at least admire a farm."

And she wrote, *Why am I so glad that he hates someone? What is in my head? He is so much older, and his skin so white and mine so brown. And even more than that, my family is poor. Why can I not stop dreaming? My heart aches from these dreams.*

And no one knew of her love for him, but God.

She saw him from the window of the living room as she cleaned. He was coming toward the house. Her heart leaped. No one was here but her. Not his mother, nor hers. What would she say to him if she finally had the courage to speak? What would she do? Never had she been alone in a room with him. But she wanted him to notice her. She would not hide. *Do not be shy anymore*, she told her crazy heart.

From the kitchen, the door slammed. His rapid footsteps came to where she was in the living room. She put down her cleaning rag and waited, just to say hello. The first time ever she would speak to him. *Look calm*, she commanded of herself. *Don't look weak or scared.*

She managed a smile as he approached.

"Good morning," she said.

He walked on past, not even slowing down or looking her way.

She heard drawers opening and closing in the bedroom nearby. The closet door slammed, curses were mumbled, then more drawers opened and closed.

Footsteps came from the hallway as he entered the living room again.

"Hello," she said as he walked on past her. Again he did not slow down or look her way.

She wrote that night in her journal. *Pay no mind to* el Patrón. *He has no heart for sympathy. His hair and skin are pale and empty while mine have the color and substance of the mother earth which grows the cotton that clothes us and the food that nourishes us. Upon the dark, rich, brown earth of paradise, God blew life and perfection into Adam and Eve to create the human race.*

And no one ever knew of her love for him, but God.

Pinochle

by

Brenda Whiteside

1961

"We saw *Return to Peyton Place* last night. I guess I'll open with fifty." Maureen gave the movie report along with her bid in the pinochle game. "What a good movie."

"You mean sexy." Ethel's round face cracked a smile as she tapped her cards on the table.

"That movie's kind of obscene." Liz narrowed her eyes in Maureen's direction. "Fifty-one. You didn't take the kids, did you?" She put a prissy, manicured finger to her thin lips.

"You guys see every new movie that comes out," Patty whined. "I can't ever get Dave to the drive-in." She folded her hand, her pink lips in a pout. "I'll have to pass."

Maureen shook her head. "No, we didn't take the kids." Liz could be such a tight-ass. "I *love* going to the drive-in. And Mike doesn't mind, as long as he can ogle women like sexy Tuesday Weld. Of course, Mike says Marilyn is his favorite."

"Aren't you bothered when your husband drools over a sexy movie star?" Liz asked. "Don't you feel a little jealous?"

"Oh, pl-lease."

"Dave's never been jealous." Patty sighed and fluffed her short, dark curls. "I sometimes wish he would be."

Ethel examined her cards. "Jealousy is *not* a good

thing. You should be happy Dave isn't the jealous type. I better say fifty-one. And who brought the chicken sandwiches today?"

"Patty already said fifty-one, and I did, and you can't be hungry already." Maureen snickered. If one thing ranked higher than sex on Ethel's list, food claimed the spot.

"Well, I am, and I'll pass."

"This hand stinks. I'll pass." Maureen leaned back and studied Patty. "You want Dave to be jealous? What if Dave was like Phil? You know Phil and Joan, don't you, Ethel?" She turned to her plump friend.

Liz interrupted. "Ethel isn't missing anything if she doesn't know them."

"I've met them a couple of times." She didn't look up from her cards. "Patty's told me a few stories. He sounds like a creep."

"He might be a creep, but he looks like Cary Grant." While visions of her favorite actor came to mind, Maureen rearranged her cards. "Oh crap, I missed that card. I could've bid again."

"Too late." Patty spread her run on the table. "He's no Cary Grant. I got the bid. Spades. He's a control freak. Joan can't even go to the store without informing him where and when she'll be back. He's so jealous she can't wear anything that shows off her figure. *And…*" She leaned in as if divulging the juiciest of gossip. "He's a sex maniac."

Ethel let go a belly laugh. "I could handle a sex maniac. Jerry thinks I'm a nymphomaniac."

"Oh, Ethel." Patty laughed. "You're awful. You wouldn't want it the way Phil is. Joan says it's like rape every time."

"Patty, please." Liz cringed and covered her face.

"Well, I'm glad Dave isn't into it like that. In fact, he's hardly into it at all…except after parties." Patty glanced around the table. "It's the weirdest thing, really. Maybe it's the alcohol or dancing with all you lovely women, but he's a go-getter after we party."

"Tell me more." Ethel's round face lit up. "Let's have the details."

Patty laughed. "I'll say one thing. I'm glad we don't party more often."

"Why do you say that?" Ethel frowned, then winked at Maureen. "You don't enjoy it at all?"

"It's usually too much trouble." She threw down the ace of hearts. "But anyway, I was thinking if Dave were ever jealous, maybe I'd feel like I have something special." Her gaze drifted above their heads. "Like maybe he really cares about me. Does that make sense?"

Patty's question wedged between the cards and settled heavily on the table.

Maureen's heart pinched for her friend, and she couldn't answer.

Ethel rearranged the cards in her hand.

Liz gently cleared her throat and squirmed in her chair before breaking the silence. "Yes. That makes sense…but Dave just isn't the jealous type. I don't think it's any reflection on you."

Maureen nodded her head in agreement, glad for the positive twist Liz found. "And jealousy is about possession. Doesn't have the slightest thing to do with love. Mike says *real* men don't get jealous."

"You're probably about the sexiest one here." Ethel's round face smiled admiringly at her. "How does Mike handle that?"

Maureen's pride puffed inwardly at the compliment. Ethel's bright eyes set too close together in her plump face. She glanced at Liz who had wavy auburn hair and dark-lashed eyes that gazed at her from a painfully thin face. Patty, cute not sensuous, embodied the darling little girl next door. "Mike doesn't have anything to handle," she demurred.

"Now, don't be coy." Ethel's admonishment jarred her.

"I've always thought Mike encouraged you to look sexy." Liz sounded accusatory. "Am I wrong?"

"No, you're right." Her husband had cut-and-dried ideas about how women should dress. "He used to buy me sexy nighties. And he always wants me to wear tight shorts and skirts. He's never been jealous. Mike says if men look at me, it makes him feel good."

"I heard something." Patty nudged her. "No more sexy nighties?"

"Running a business and raising kids can be distracting," Maureen countered. They both claimed exhaustion at times, but the bedroom hadn't become a dead zone yet.

Liz glanced at each of the women. "I think the old sex life calms down after fifteen years of marriage."

"Oh hell, no." Maureen blurted out. Everyone laughed. "Maybe after sixteen years and buying a business, but even then…it ain't that bad."

"Care to share the details?" Patty's pink lips formed a kiss.

"Whoa, boy." Maureen laughed. "Alfred Kinsey should've interviewed our pinochle group."

****

1962   '

"Here we go." Maureen dealt the last card. She glanced out the window when the dog barked. "What's the latest this week?"

"My little Eric says he's going to fly to the moon when he grows up." Liz smiled as she arranged the cards in her hand. "I'll open with fifty."

"The moon." Maureen groaned. Current events bored her. "That's all they've been talking about at my house lately. Ever since someone flew around it or something."

"John Glenn." Ethel frowned at her cards. "I'll pass."

"Yes, I guess that was his name. Anyway, Annie says when she grows up, she wants to go to the moon, too. And Mike says, why not? Mike says this is the best thing to happen to America in a long time."

"It's pretty exciting. Even romantic." Liz breathed the word like a sigh. "Fly me to the moon."

"There are times I could send Jerry to the moon, and it isn't for romance." Ethel laughed.

"Romance. What do *husbands* know about romance?" Patty smirked at her friends. "I'll pass, too."

"You've got that right, Patty." Ethel nodded. "Jerry thinks romance is asking me if I want a roll in the hay. I made tuna macaroni salad, so speak up when you get hungry."

"Why do I get such crappy hands?" Maureen rearranged her cards. "Pass. Jerry can't be that awful. You have four children, for goodness' sake, and you've been married quite a few years."

"Okay then, ladies. I get it cheap for fifty," Liz said. "Hearts."

Ethel moaned. "You would say hearts. Eh. Jerry

isn't awful. I like to joke about him, but don't get me wrong—he's no Don Juan in the libido department. Lower than I'd like. But I can't honestly complain. He's good and faithful. I certainly don't have to worry about him straying."

"And would it be so awful if he did?" Patty gave a sideways glance.

Maureen considered her friend. What was with her today? She seemed fidgety.

"Course it would be." Ethel tossed a card on the table. "No woman wants a man that can't keep his pants on."

"Men aren't the only ones who stray." Articles about movie actress affairs with handsome co-stars could be found in the pages of the magazines Maureen loved to read. "Women have affairs, too."

Patty shot her a look and continued quizzing Ethel. "I don't mean all the time. What if Jerry had one indiscretion?"

"It's hardly worth the debate. He doesn't have enough for me. He certainly couldn't get it up enough to cheat on me."

Everyone laughed.

"But if it did ever happen…" A dark grimace replaced the usual sweetness on Ethel's round face. "I'd make the bastard pay."

"What if *you* had an affair?" Patty asked Ethel. "You're always complaining about not getting enough. Haven't you ever been tempted to have an affair? You do like your sex, Ethel."

"Jerry would probably be glad. Take the pressure off him."

Maureen laughed. "Oh, Ethel, really." She'd read

about open marriage. Was it possible her lusty friend would consider such a thing?

"But as far as I'm concerned…" Ethel glanced around the table, seeming to give each of them her full attention. "I'd rather keep it in my own backyard."

Maureen turned her gaze on Patty as she spoke. "They say there's hardly a couple around that one or the other partner doesn't stray once in the marriage. A high percentage of women do." Her cute-as-the-girl-next-door friend had some sort of secret. Would she spill? Patty narrowed her eyes, and Maureen smiled back.

"Would anyone like coffee?" Liz rose and went to the kitchen.

Maureen shook her head and continued. "This article said women need and enjoy sex every bit as much as men. And a high percentage of women go outside the marriage and have affairs."

Patty ignored her and turned back to Ethel. "But if you had an affair, wouldn't Jerry be forgiving, for the sake of the marriage and the children? If it's only sex?"

"He'd never know," Ethel answered. "Hell, I could have a couple of affairs going and still have enough left over for Jerry."

"Mike would know if I had an affair." Maureen would never be able to hide betrayal. Her husband knew her too well.

"And if you had one little indiscretion, wouldn't Mike forgive you? If you ever found someone else irresistible and, well, you know, romantic? He'd forgive you because with you and Mike, love would win out." Patty's bottom lip pouted as if jealous of what she and Mike had.

"I had an affair." Liz stood in the kitchen doorway

with a coffee cup in her hand. Her lids fluttered over liquid, dark eyes. She dropped her chin, and her thin frame heaved a sigh.

The three women gaped in silent shock.

Patty seized the silence. "And you're still together. Your marriage survived."

"You do get over it." Liz glanced at her friends. "And, anyway, this happened a couple of years ago. Just after we had Stevie. Allen and I had trouble coping with a new baby. Not much intimacy. I felt…neglected."

"Who? How long?" Patty probed.

"Patty, really," Maureen admonished. "That's none of our business."

Liz waved them off, dismissing Patty's inquisitiveness. "No one you know. I saw him only a couple of times, and the guilt got to me. We settled into our baby years, and Allen never found out." She set the tray of coffee cups on the table and sat.

"Just like that?" Ethel asked incredulously.

"Now, Ethel." Patty's pug nose lifted with smugness as if she'd found absolution in Liz's confession. "A good marriage withstands little indiscretions. Sex certainly isn't all there is to marriage."

"It sure beats whatever's in second."

Liz gave a tight smile, and Patty snickered.

Maureen surveyed Liz. She sat rod-straight, but something in her face appeared a touch more relaxed than usual. Patty's self-satisfied grin remained. "It's your play, Patty." She brought them back to the game. "Did you hear the latest on Marilyn Monroe's death?"

****

1963

"I can't concentrate today." Maureen rearranged her

cards for the third time.

"Then pass, sweetie, and let's keep the game going." Ethel sounded less than sympathetic.

Patty turned to Ethel, speaking as if Maureen wasn't in the room. "She sat in front of that television all day yesterday and watched him get shot over and over again."

"This is the end of Camelot. What's Jackie going to do?" Maureen sighed. "And poor little John-John." Her heart ached for his fatherless children; the handsome president and his wife's fairy-tale life had come to an abrupt finale.

"Pass, would you?" Ethel snapped. "I have a killer hand."

"All right. All right, but no table talk. I pass." She loved Ethel, but the woman's lack of sentimentality could be annoying.

"Sixty!"

"Pass." Liz's voice was barely audible.

"You got it, partner." Patty smiled at Ethel. "Listen, Maureen, we understand the tragedy. The whole world's in shock. But don't *dwell* on it."

"They were such a perfect couple."

"Oh, blah," Ethel scoffed. "No such thing."

"And those darling children being raised without a daddy." His toothy grin, images of him tossing his son in the air, and that movie star square jaw wouldn't leave her thoughts.

"Ham sandwiches." Ethel looked at Liz. "You made ham sandwiches, didn't you?"

Liz nodded without looking up.

"I thought so. I can smell them. Is it lunchtime yet?"

"You're right about one thing, Maureen. Our

problems seem small in comparison," Patty conceded.

"Not really." Liz's voice floated, barely more than a whisper. Everyone watched and waited. "That's on TV."

"Yes, Liz. And?" Patty pried.

"Karen got caught smoking pot behind the Palm Theater yesterday."

"Your daughter? Oh my gosh. Oh noooo," Maureen gushed, grabbing Liz's hand. "Is she in jail?"

"No, no." Liz's eyes grew watery.

"Tell us what happened, for God's sake." Patty folded her cards.

"She and her friends. One of the parents caught them. She's only fifteen." Liz wrung her hands.

"Oh, hon." Maureen patted her arm.

Liz sniffed. "She's grounded."

"She's *grounded?*" Ethel drew her chin back and frowned. "That's it?"

"Of course, that's not *it*." Her eyes slanted downward, giving her already thin face a gaunt appearance.

"No, of course not." Maureen squeezed her hand. "Mike says talking to your kids is the best way to keep them out of trouble. You and Allen will get her back in line." She ventured a smile. "Is she addicted?"

Ethel laughed. "Maureen, really. Don't scare poor Liz. Marijuana isn't like heroine."

Liz's head jerked. "Like what?"

"Do you want to go home, Liz? Skip the cards for today?" Patty asked.

"No. I'd rather be with you guys." She smiled weakly.

"Okay, then. Let's play." Ethel picked up her cards. "And let's eat lunch early today."

Maureen sighed, happy to have good children and to not have Ethel's appetite.

****

1964

"The girls are driving me crazy with wanting to go to California this summer." Maureen sorted her cards. "They think they'll see the Beach Boys or something."

"I get that." Patty grinned. "Dave and I are going to the coast for a long weekend next month. I'll open with fifty-one."

"Oh good, partner." Ethel was pleased. "I can use that."

"Hey, no table talk," Maureen joked.

"Without the kids? Just you and Dave?" Liz frowned and spoke quietly.

Patty beamed. "Yep."

Ethel studied Liz for a moment. "Are you okay today? You look kind of pale."

Liz nodded her head without looking up from her cards.

"Mike says we should go somewhere without the girls, but I don't know when." Maureen thought his idea more of a wish than reality. They rarely took vacations. Leaving the girls at home if they did go somewhere wouldn't be fair. "How'd you talk Dave into that?"

"Oh, I have my ways."

"Honestly, Patty, your ways have certainly been working lately." Ethel laughed. "I've seen the florist deliver to you twice in the last week, and that ain't glass you're wearing around your wrist."

"Diamonds are a girl's best friend," Maureen sang. "Fifty-two. Patty does seem persuasive lately."

Liz squirmed in her chair. "Can we play cards?"

"Sixty." Ethel smiled. "No use pussyfooting."

"Pass." Liz sighed.

"What's the secret?" Ethel pursued. "All we hear from you is how Dave is anything but attentive."

"I guess men can change," Maureen offered, running interference for Patty on this line of questioning.

"Sure, when they feel guilty." Ethel laughed. "I brought egg salad sandwiches. Is it lunchtime yet?"

"Are you ever not hungry, Ethel?" Maureen wanted to counsel her on her expanding waistline, but thought better.

"No." Ethel threw off the intended jab and concentrated on Patty. "So is he feeling guilty? Come on, Liz. Help me on this. Maureen seems to know what is going on, but we don't."

Liz tucked her chin closer to her chest and didn't answer.

"Liz?" Ethel looked puzzled.

"Really none of our business." Liz shook her head.

Maureen watched Patty fidget with her cards and answered for her. "I think Patty and Dave are renewing the romance in their marriage."

"Do we have to talk about this…I mean romance, today?" Liz's eyes watered as she rearranged her cards yet again.

"What is the matter with you today, Liz?" Patty asked.

Liz shook her head and looked out the window.

"Well, I want to know what's up." Ethel folded her cards and glared at Maureen and Patty.

"Oh, what the hell?" Patty glanced at Maureen and smirked. "I think, Ethel, you'd call it making the bastard pay."

Liz gasped.

Ethel's mouth fell open.

"Hey, it was last month. Old news. What's trump?"

"So, Mike says we're taking the girls to Malibu. Where are you and Dave going?" Maureen helped her change the subject.

"Haven't decided yet."

"Now, just wait a minute." Ethel finally found her voice. "Is that it? Is that all we're going to get? How did you find out? Do you know who she was?"

"I'm not feeling so well." Liz started to stand up.

"No, I do not know who, and I do—not—care. I haven't had this much attention from my husband since we were single, and he spent a month of dates to get my undies off in the back seat of his Chevy."

"He didn't tell you who she was?" Liz rubbed her eyes and sat back down.

Patty continued. "Nope. And, anyway, I took the advice you offered oh so long ago, Ethel. You spoke wisdom. Make the bastard pay." She grinned. "And life goes on."

"Well, in that case"—Ethel's round face remained stoic—"your station wagon could be replaced with a new Mustang."

Silence fell like a blanket over the women. Outside a dog barked. Maureen glanced out the window where the leaves on the trees shivered in the cold wind. "I guess happily ever after isn't black and white."

"Not too many things are," Patty said.

"Except maybe the newspaper and old movies on TV." Maureen glanced around the table and forced a smile.

"And the black and white sundaes Ethel loves," Liz

added, her gaze not meeting the others but her voice stronger.

"And Sammy Davis Jr. and May Britt." Patty giggled.

"And my pinochle hand." Ethel spread out her run in clubs.

The sun split the clouds, sending a shaft of light across the table. Maureen snuck a peek at each of the women at the table and wondered about the grayness of happily ever after.

The Tuesday Night Meeting

by

Peggy Jaeger

"The October 19 meeting of the Tuesday Night Ladies Club is officially called to order," Mavis Carruthers declared in her rich, deep voice. "The secretary will please read the minutes from the previous meeting."

Suellen Jones stood and patted her freshly permed silver hair that she'd had done-up that morning down at Maybelle's Beauty Emporium. She cleared her throat once, then began. "The October 5 meeting took place in the home of June Jackson with MaryLee Cranston and Cassandra Beatty co-hostessing. Sixteen members were present. After a delicious sampling of Clara Mark's homemade apple spice and lemon cake, the meeting was called to order."

Suellen's lyrical voice sang throughout the small room. Thirty-odd years as a fifth grade English teacher had taught her the importance of a voice that didn't lull the listener to sleep.

"We currently have over two thousand dollars in our savings account, according to treasurer Peggy Nelson. She'll be a little late tonight, by the way, Madam President."

Mavis nodded. The club treasurer's tardiness was a common occurrence.

"Some suggestions on what to do with the available funds was discussed," Suellen continued, "and the general consensus was we wait until the Christmas donation requests come in to see who we can help the most."

The members present looked around at one another and nodded in agreement at the soundness of the decision.

"A condolence card was sent to Bertha Magnussen on the death of her beloved daughter, Beatrice. A few members were able to attend the service and said Bea looked lovely."

"You'da never known she had cancer," Molly Kane interrupted. "That new makeup girl at Upson's Funeral Parlor did quite a job on Bea."

Suellen smiled blandly at Molly. Everyone had grown used to the woman's interjections.

Suellen continued. "Under new business, one name was put up for membership and was voted favorably upon." She looked over the sheet in her hand at the audience of faces before her. "Most of you know Cora Patterly."

A sea of nodding heads met her eyes. Yes, they all knew Cora.

And her husband, Bob.

"An invitation was extended to Cora to attend tonight's meeting. She called me this morning and said she'd be here about seven thirty. That'll give us all a chance to sit and chat with her."

Wisteria Plowright raised her withered hand.

"Yes, Wisteria?" Mavis asked.

Standing on spindly, varicosed legs with the support of a marble-headed cane, the oldest member of the club asked, in a voice barely above a breathless whisper, "Madam President, does Cora know anything about the purpose of our group?"

"To my knowledge, no," Mavis answered. "But I

think when she discovers our purpose and realizes all the good we do, she'll be more than happy to join us."

As if on cue, the doorbell to Rachel Down's house sounded. Always the most gracious of hostesses, Rachel sprang to the door, opening it before the bell even completed its chime.

"Cora!" she greeted, a smile widening on her happy and welcoming face. "We're so glad you could join us tonight."

Entering the spacious living room, Cora Patterly's gaze shifted from Rachel to the faces of the other women present.

From a cursory glance, all the ladies present were in their daily finest unlike the drab, dowdy way she was dressed. A once white, now gray, long-sleeved blouse hung loosely from her stooped shoulders. It was tucked into an elastic-waisted, calf-length shirt that had been in fashion fifteen years prior. The left leg of her pantyhose had a visible run spiraling upward from the ankle, and she hadn't had a spare moment to change into a fresh pair before leaving her house. Her brown bow-tie shoes badly needed new laces and soles, too. Cora had a fairly good idea of what she looked like in her old Salvation Army store-bought clothes. Though only thirty-six, most people thought her a score older.

"I-I'm sorry I'm late," she said, clasping her weathered handbag to her chest, her hands shaking with nerves. "Bob was late coming home, and I didn't want to leave the kids alone."

Mavis Carruthers smiled and said, "Well, you're here now, and that's what counts, Cora. Come in and have a taste of Rachel's famous blueberry pecan pie."

Rachel led Cora to a high-backed chair strategically

placed between Mavis and the club's vice president Kathryn Anne Swayze. Cora was then given a tray with a large helping of pie and a coffee cup.

"Would you care for coffee, Cora, or tea?" Rachel asked, illuminating the room with her brilliant smile.

"Coffee, please, and thank you kindly for the pie. I didn't get a chance to have much supper before I came here. The diner was near to bursting with customers this evening."

Trays were passed around, and coffee abundantly poured. As she sipped the heavenly tasting brew, Cora's attention was grabbed by Wisteria Plowright.

"Cora, my dear, we are all so pleased you could join us tonight."

"Thank you, Miz Plowright. I was honored to be asked, although, I don't rightly know why I was."

A few members slid side glances at one another. Their knowing looks added to Cora's state of nerves.

"We'll get to that, dear," Suellen said. "First, we'd all like to sit and visit with you a while. Get to know you a little more and have you know us better, too."

"Understand your eldest, Jemima, is on the honor roll this year at the junior high," Meadly Carson said.

If it was possible for Cora Patterly to beam, she did right then, pride flowing through her. "Yes, ma'am, she is. I'm…we're…so proud of her. Second in her class, too."

"I'd be proud as well," Kathryn Anne put in. "Your girl has a lot of potential. She'll go far in the world if she's given the right chances."

"Now, your youngest, Paul," Meadly continued. "I hear from my grandson, Jackson, your Paul's got a real fine aptitude for those computers that are all the rage nowadays."

"Yes, ma'am, he does," Cora said, finally relaxing, content to show her pride in her children, the one bright spot in her otherwise bleak life. "The schools are real up now on computer learning. Paul tells me they even have their own language and all."

"Imagine that," Wisteria exclaimed, sipping her heavily laced tea.

"You certainly have done a fine job with those two, Cora," Mavis said.

"Thank you, Miz Carruthers," Cora replied, tears brimming. "It hasn't been easy."

"Don't suppose it has, seeing as you've had to contend with the no-account they have for a father," Molly Kane commented.

The room went silent. Mavis shot Molly daggers from across the room, the slice of which the older woman ignored.

"Bob tries his best, Miz Kane. Honest he does," Cora said, her cheeks heating. "He means well, but…well…he…"

As she trailed off, Wisteria rose and hobbled over to Cora's side. Kathryn Anne graciously gave up her chair for the oldest member and founder of the club. Wisteria settled in and took Cora's work-weary hand in her own gnarled one. "My dear, sometimes we can be confronted by truths which are hard to acknowledge. I know Molly didn't mean to upset you. We would never insult a guest, especially one we want to join our organization."

Blinking back tears, Cora replied, "That's all right, Miz Plowright. I know no harm was intended. My Bob, well, he's just high-strung's all."

"High-strung," Molly repeated and crossed her arms

over her ample bosom. "Better *strung up*, I say."

Cora's trembling returned. "Now, Miz Kane, I can understand why you feel that way and all, with the problems you've had with Bob. I apologize for the trouble he's caused you."

"No need for you to apologize, Cora," Molly said. She peered through her thick eyeglasses and continued. "The fault's not yours. You're a lot like your mother, God rest her soul. Forgiving and apologizing all the time for things beyond her."

"Bob means well, honest he does," Cora said, her eyes pleading at the women in the room. "It's, well, he can't seem to find his way."

"Is that any reason for him to hit you and the children, Cora?" Mavis asked, her sonorous voice booming accusingly throughout the room.

Cora's eyes widened, bulging against the sockets. Before she could deny the charge, Mavis silenced her with a wave of her hand.

"That bruise over your left cheek is mostly faded now. It's been three weeks since you were seen in the emergency room over at County General. Kitty Hawkins was the night supervisor on duty the evening you were brought in. You told some cock-and-bull tale about falling down the basement steps. The story was as phony as the blood on your dress was real. You don't have a basement. The sheriff hauled Bob in for the night and charged him with disturbing the peace and public drunkenness. I can only imagine what small, insignificant thing you did that he thought you deserved a beating for."

The little of Cora's remaining will dissolved under the older woman's gaze. A flood of tears poured out of her all at once, and a sob rocked her chest.

Kathryn Anne provided a lace handkerchief, as Wisteria patted Cora's arm.

"It's all right, darlin'. You're among friends here."

Cora swiped at her eyes. "I'm...I'm sorry for the blubbering, ladies. Truly I am. It's just been so hard. With Bob scraping from one job to the next...never enough money for food. He drinks to try and forget his troubles, his failures. But I swear on my mother's soul, Miz Carruthers, he's never laid a hand on the children. He wouldn't dare."

"We believe you, my dear," Wisteria said. Taking a deep breath, she added, "I think now might be a good time to tell you about our organization, about why we asked you here tonight." She looked up at the current president of the club.

"Cora," Mavis aid, capturing the entire attention of the room, "do you know anything about our group?"

She shook her head and swiped at her still running nose. "Not much, ma'am. I know you give out scholarships to worthy high school girls for college. And you support the poor, especially at the holidays. I've seen write-ups in the paper about the good things y'all have done. But aside from those, I don't know much else. Excepting," she said, " that you're all widows."

The members of the club collectively smiled at her.

"That's why I thought it strange to be asked here tonight. I'm not a widow."

"No, darlin', you're not," Wisteria said, smiling. "Not yet."

Cora gaped, openmouthed, at the old woman.

"Let me start at the beginning, dear, so you'll understand how our little club came to be."

Settling back in the chair, Wisteria took a breath, then began her tale.

"You probably don't remember my late husband, Major Plowright. I believe he passed when you were just a baby. Well, my dear, if there was ever a tougher man in the world to live with, I'd be sore pressed to believe it. I truly feel the moment he was brought into the world a military angel crossed his path and predestined him for a soldier's life. His mother told me after we'd been married for about a year that even as a child, everything had to be precision perfect in his world. He tolerated no fools, silliness, or any kind of good-natured fun. I didn't realize this when I married him, mind you. I know now I fell in love with his spit and polish exterior and superior manner. I never could resist a good-lookin' man in a uniform."

A few knowing chuckles escaped throughout the room.

"Well, married life was kind of sweet for a while. I got used to his ranting and raving about precision and cleanliness and order. But when the Major was forced to retire at a very early age, well, it all changed. He changed. Nothing I did was ever good enough. I was plum worn out with three babies and a big house to care for, and he never helped a lick with anything. One day he came home from his club and my youngest had spilled his juice all over the kitchen floor. I was just about to clean it up, but the Major didn't let me. He stormed into the room, saw the mess, and started screaming and hollering so loud I thought my little Jimmy's diapers were gonna fall off. When I tried to explain about the mess, he smacked me across the face. Knocked me clear across the kitchen with one fell swoop of the back of his hand. I was so stunned, I didn't see the next one coming. He was raving about me being an inadequate wife and mother and that he was going to teach me a lesson I'd never forget. He was right about it, too. I never forgot that first beating or all the others he gave me after. I do believe he came to enjoy it when he struck me down. I'd see a gleam in his eyes, kind of like the one I'd seen when he was in the throes of passion, whenever he hit me." Wisteria stopped and refreshed herself with a sip of tea.

"Miz Plowright, ma'am. I had no idea," Cora said.

"Of course not, darlin'. In those days, why, a woman was barely a step above chattel. Men's property, bought and sold."

"What did you do? I mean, did you stay with the Major?"

"For a while. I ran away with the children once, to my mother. But the Major followed me and dragged us all back. The beating I endured that night broke my left arm and two of my ribs."

"I remember he went around town the next day telling everyone who'd listen that you fell down the front steps because you were rushing off somewhere in a dither," Molly Kane said.

When Cora gasped, Wisteria patted her hand sand said, "You see, Cora. We've all lied at one time or another about our bruises."

"Finish your story, Wisteria," Mavis commanded.

After taking another sip of tea, she did. "I knew I had to do something about the situation, but what? I couldn't leave him. He'd shown me how he'd hunt me down and bring me back. Divorce was out of the question in those days. No self-respectin' woman of the South would ever be seen in divorce court, airing all her

49

dirty personal laundry. I finally figured out I had two options. I could stay and put up with this man I'd grown to fear and hate until he finally succeeded in killing me, or…"

"Or?" Cora prompted.

"Or I could rid myself and the children of him right then and there."

Cora's loud intake of air was the one sound in the room. To the question in her eyes, Wisteria merely inclined her head.

"Yes, my dear. I killed my husband. It was the only way I could survive."

"But…but how? I mean…why weren't you caught? Arrested? I don't understand." Cora's voice took on a sudden high-pitched, hysterical note.

Recognizing the signs, Wisteria grabbed Cora's hand and squeezed it. Hard. "I know you have a million questions, Cora dear. All will be answered, but please, let me finish first."

Cora, her eyes still wide, nodded.

"I had to make it look like an accident, I knew that much. The Major provided me with the perfect outlet. You see, after he'd retired from active service, he had trouble sleeping through the night. He began going down to his study at all odd hours, having a few glasses of port, and then returning to bed. The alcohol helped lull him to sleep. One night he tripped coming up the stairs. I believe he must have had a little more than usual, and an idea suddenly wormed its way into my head. What of he fell down those stairs while drunk? Would it kill him? I counted the number of steps the next day. There were seventeen. I'll remember that number for the rest of my life. Seventeen steps from top to bottom; seventeen steps to freedom.

"That night I lay awake, hoping the Major was doing the same. We had separate bedrooms in those days. Luckily, he *was* having some trouble. When I heard him get up, put on his robe and slippers, and go out into the hall, I knew my chance had come. I sneaked out behind him and watched as he went into his study. I waited at the top of the stairs for over an hour. My legs started to cramp, and after a bit I feared he'd fallen asleep in one of the chairs. But then I heard him coming. I watched, hidden by the shadows, from the top riser. The moment he placed his foot upon the final step, I leapt out of my hiding spot and pushed him hard as I could in the chest. I knew I'd have just one opportunity to see this through. If I failed, then the Major would surely kill me."

She took another long pull of her tea. "My strength did me proud as he toppled backward. He tried to grab hold of the banister, but I slapped his hand away before he could latch on. He cried out once, a sound I will never forget. The next thing I knew he was sprawled out on the foyer floor. I had to go down those seventeen steps to make sure he wasn't breathing. I tell you, Cora dear, nothing has ever terrified me more. Well, he must have broken his neck during the fall, because it was at a pretty peculiar angle. When I made sure he wasn't breathing and that his pulse had stopped, I called the sheriff straight away, then Old Doc Higgins, bless his heart. Pronounced the Major dead at the scene, declared it an accident, since he'd had such a high alcohol content in his blood. From that day to this, I've been free. And no one has ever known the truth outside of this circle of women here tonight."

"But weren't you afraid, I mean, didn't you think

someone would…"

"Would what, my dear? Tell my secret?" Wisteria smiled knowingly, her eyes dilating as she scanned the faces in the room. "No, I'm not worried. You see, we all have out little secrets here."

The full realization of Wisteria Plowright's words became crystal clear to Cora. Her mouth fell open as she looked each woman in the eyes.

They were smiling back at her, some nodding to her unasked question.

"But…but *you,* Miz Johnson? And you, Miz Kane?" Cora cried.

"Done mine with cyanide," Molly stated. "Stank like almonds in my sitting room for a week."

"I can't believe this." Cora shot up from her chair. And then the reason she'd been invited to the meeting washed through her.

"Oh! *OH!*" She grabbed the arm of her chair for support, terrified she would fall to her knees at the weight of the knowledge about why these women wanted her here.

"Now, Cora," Mavis said. "Just calm yourself for a minute, and I'll finish the story for you. I think when you hear the rest you'll understand everything better."

Hands and legs still shaking like laundry line-drying in the afternoon breeze, Cora eased back into the chair.

"Now, right after the Major's death, June Jackson, who'd been a neighbor of the Plowrights', came to Wisteria one day in tears. Seems she suffered through a lot with her Albert too, like Wisteria had. June didn't know which way to turn, so Wisteria confided what she'd done to the Major, and June thought it sounded like a pretty good idea to her. Well, to make a long story short, Albert Jackson died of a heart attack one month later. Since he'd had a history of heart trouble, it was ruled natural causes. Only Wisteria and June knew it was from the overdose of foxglove she'd put in his tea one night after dinner. The other name for foxglove, my dear, you may know is digitalis. A very potent heart medication."

Cora's breathing went shallow as Mavis finished the tale.

"After that, the two friends decided to start a club, of sorts, made up of women who were known to be abused by their men. Remember, it wasn't called spousal abuse in those days like it is now. The club blossomed and grew. We've all lived with the torture of beatings and abuse and because our judicial system is negligent in how it protects women, we've had to resort to our own special brand of justice. And that," Mavis said, taking Cora's ice-cold hands, "is why we invited you here tonight. We all know about Bob Patterly and his drunken, no-account, abusing ways. We've all witnessed at one time or another how he's treated you in public. And we don't need to imagine what goes on behind the closed doors of your home. If your dear mother were alive, she'd tell you the same thing we are. Get rid of him, Cora. Get him out of your life now before he kills you. Get him out of your life for good."

Cora stared hard at Mavis, digesting all of the woman's words. It was too true her life had been a hell on earth for more years than she could remember. She could never leave him, though. She too, like Wisteria, had tried once. Bob had found her and beaten her unconscious. No, she couldn't leave. She was trapped the same way all these fine women had been.

Only now they were free.

But was it worth the price she might pay if she got caught?

"How?" she asked, meekly, still staring at Mavis. "How can I do something like this?"

A cacophony of suggestions flew at her from left and right.

"Poison," Anne Jorgenson said.

"Hot rig his car," proclaimed Dotty Marshall.

"Leave a burning cigarette at his bedside," Kathryn Anne added.

"No, that's not what I mean," Cora cried. "How can I do something like you're all suggesting and not possibly get caught? What would happen to my children? To me?"

"I wouldn't worry too much about that, Cora dear," Wisteria commented as the front doorbell chimed.

As Rachel ran to answer it, Cora asked, "But what about the sheriff? I'm sure to be found out if I kill Bob. The sheriff will arrest me as sure as I'm sitting here."

"Sorry I'm late," Peggy Nelson said, entering the room. "I got tied up at a huge traffic accident out on the highway."

"*Sheriff Nelson*," Cora screeched, her hand flying to her breast.

"Cora," Peggy Nelson, current sheriff of Bowman's County and treasurer of the Tuesday Night Club said, smiling. She took both of Cora's hands in her own and said, "I'm so glad you could join us tonight."

911, What's Your Emergency?

by

D. V. Stone

This story is dedicated to the men and women who run toward danger instead of away. I hope it gives you, the reader, a small peek inside the life of First Responders—people who give up sleep, time with family, and holidays. Next time you see red-and-blue lights, I'd like you to remember the men and women who are manning the front line, which is often the line between life and death.

Monday nights were usually crazy busy at the Slate Quarry Volunteer Ambulance Company. Shay McDowell had a gut feeling that night would be no exception. When the first call came in, she'd barely finished going over the equipment check sheet. Once the clipboard was stowed in the cabinet, she climbed up front into the passenger seat. On the other side of the windshield, Joanna slapped the big red button and opened the bay door. Whirring noises from the mechanism filled the garage while her partner yanked the charging cord from the side of the ambulance. By the time the door was all the way up, her partner had jumped into the driver's side and clicked her seat belt.

Northeastern Pennsylvania Dispatch relayed the information, and Shay started the call sheet on a non-responsive diabetic. Sometimes a person with diabetes didn't realize until too late that their sugar level was low. At that point, they couldn't help themselves. First, the patient began to sweat, and then confusion took over. If left untreated, the diabetic could have seizures and even die.

"Hopefully, someone on the scene has glucose gel or a glucagon injector." Joanna adjusted the mirror, hit the lights, and pulled out.

Zach stood by the side of the door, ready to close it behind them.

"Does he ever go home?"

"Nope, at least not very often." Shay glanced out her

window and down the road. "It's clear this way."

Joanna pulled the rig out into the chilly October day. At the stop sign she made a left after a pickup blew through, disregarding the ambulance's lights and sirens. "Jerk."

By the time they got to the scene, the patient did indeed have glucagon. He was sitting up in the chair, talking to another first responder.

"Sorry for the trouble." The patient gave a sheepish smile

It's no trouble," Alex replied, stowing away his gear. "Are you sure you don't want to go and get checked out?"

"Hey, Alex." Shay stooped next to the chair while tucking a stray piece of chestnut-brown hair behind her ear. "What's going on?"

"This is Mr. Peters. He was busy and forgot to eat, so his glucose levels dropped. Luckily, his wife was with him and dosed him with glucagon. He's declining medical treatment at this time."

The man's color was good, and he wasn't sweating. Shay turned from her assessment when his wife entered the room with a glass of orange juice and some cheese and crackers. "You're sure about us not taking you in for a quick look over?"

"I'm sure. Sorry for the trouble, but my wife and I can handle this. Thank you for your service, but we're good." Mr. Peters glanced over at his wife and she nodded in agreement.

"Seems like you have it under control." She gave the wife a smile and wink. "And you're in capable hands."

"We've done this before." The woman set the tray down on a nearby table and placed a hand on her hip while glowering at her husband. "He gets wrapped up in his projects and doesn't listen."

The room was filled with Christmas decorations in various stages of assembly.

"This is amazing." Shay stood and walked to where blow molds of penguins stood in a line near a manger. "I guess you guys have a thing for the holidays."

"You should come back after Thanksgiving when it's all set up." Mr. Peters beamed. "I set up an outside display. Folks come from all over to check it out."

Mrs. Peters rolled her eyes. "You should check out our electric bill too."

The room filled with good-natured laughter. This couple was a riot.

Once the paperwork for refusal of transport was complete, Shay and Joanna said goodbye to Alex and headed back to base.

"How about a quick stop for coffee. I have a funny feeling it's going to be a long night."

Shay's intuition was right. They'd finish one call, and then another came in on its heels.

First up, a man who was short of breath. Then a child fell, fracturing his collarbone. The last alert was a fender bender on the highway exit ramp.

It was almost two a.m. by the time they finally made it back to the squad house.

Shay flopped onto the couch. Not even thirty seconds later, the sound of dispatch blared again. Unknown problem at a familiar address.

Joanna moaned, "Really. Tonight?"

"Come on. No rest for the wicked." Shay hauled Joanna to her feet. "Let's go, Millie needs a friend."

This time Joanna was happy to let Shay drive while

she catnapped in the passenger seat. Shay smiled, thinking about her next patient.

Millie St. Clair was an elderly woman who lived alone with her two cats, and an ancient pug named Willis. Every couple of weeks, when she couldn't sleep, she decided she was sick and called the ambulance. Millie was a sweet old lady, and usually they didn't mind reassuring her. The trip to the ER was always an easy and amusing run. Millie would chat away about her past or her pet's antics. When they turned her over to the nurses, her grandson was usually waiting to take her home.

"Joanna, wake up." Muscles knotted in Shay's neck. Millie wasn't standing at the front door waving at them as usual. She hit the brakes and slammed the lever into park. When the rig came to a halt, Shay threw the door open, jumped out, and ran to the house while Joanna grabbed their equipment. After knocking and not getting an answer, she tried the doorknob. It opened.

"Millie?" she called. As concerned as she was, she knew better than to not be cautious. "It's Shay and Joanna. Millie?"

The semi-dark hallway glowed with light from a small lamp. Nothing looked amiss as she waited for Joanna to catch up. You never went into an unknown situation without backup.

Red-and-blue lights shone through the window from a police car entering the street.

A groan came from the back of the house as Joanna came up behind her. No more waiting. Still, they moved with caution. Reaching the entryway of the kitchen, Shay paused and scanned the room. The elderly woman lay crumpled on the floor. "Millie, what happened?"

"Careful, Shay," Millie mumbled. "Willis spilled his water. The floor is slippery. That's how I fell."

Skirting the puddle, Shay reached for Millie's outstretched hand. It was so cold. "How long have you been on the floor?"

"Since right before dark. It took me a while to get over to the phone." Millie groaned again. "I couldn't get up. I dragged myself over so I could reach it."

"You poor thing." Shay patted her hand. "We're here now."

When Joanna asked someone behind them to get a blanket, Shay glanced up from her assessment.

Michael Machu, a policeman, poked his head in the door. "Hey, Shay."

"Hey, Michael." With a nod she went right back to her patient. "Where is the most pain, Millie?"

"My leg, near the top, is the worst, but my wrist hurts too."

Moving from top to bottom, Shay took extra care running her hands over the older woman's frail body. Her partner obtained their patient's vital signs, gathering the blood pressure reading and then pulse rate.

When Shay palpated the patient's wrist, Millie cried out. "Sorry, Millie." She winced. "Michael, we'll need a splint."

Then she touched lower. Millie's right leg rotated out, and it was significantly shorter than the left. The woman had most likely fractured her hip as well when she fell. "We're also going to need the longboard. How are her vitals?"

"Blood pressure is a little low, and her heart rate is up." Joanna got an oxygen mask ready. "Millie, I'm going to place this over your head and give you a little more air. Ok, sweetie?"

Michael returned with the longboard, loaded on the stretcher with blankets and the splints. "Here, I grabbed a bunch."

"Millie, I have to talk to the paramedics for a minute. I'm not going to leave you."

While Jo splinted the injured wrist, Shay reached up and keyed her mic. When the medics responded, she filled them in on the situation and patient's vitals. "Patient is a little shocky but seems stable."

Done with the report, she returned her attention to Millie. "Here's what's going to happen. The paramedics will be here in a few minutes and start an IV to give you fluids. They will attach electrodes to monitor your heart."

"Is something wrong with my heart?" Millie's eyes opened wide, and she trembled.

"No, sweetie," Joanna piped in. "That's normal procedure. Don't you worry."

Millie calmed.

The woman trusted them.

"The medics will look you over, too. Once the IV is in, we'll move you onto the big board over there, so you don't get jiggled around. It's not going to be comfortable, but we'll try our best to make you as pain-free as possible."

"What about my pets?" Millie's voice quivered.

"Don't worry. When you get to the hospital, they'll call your grandson. In the meantime, the officer will put them in your bedroom so they don't get out," Joanna reassured her.

"I'll take good care of them, ma'am." Michael had already scooped up one of the curious cats. "I have my own dogs."

Joanna crawled under the table where Willis, the cause of all the trouble, lay chewing on a rawhide. "Come on, you rascal. Time for bed."

The pug was nonchalant about the whole thing. He didn't give Joanna any trouble, even when she dragged him out. "Be right back."

With her good hand, Millie patted Shay's arm. "I pray and thank God for you girls every night before bed. I ask Him to watch over you and keep you safe."

"Thanks, Millie, we need all the prayers we can get." Shay smiled at her.

Joanna and Michael re-entered the kitchen, followed by the paramedics.

Millie was soon hooked up to the ECG machine, and her IV started.

"Ouch," Millie called out when they moved her to the board.

"Easy, Millie. Don't try to help." Shay stroked the wrinkled forehead. "Let us do the work, okay?"

Rolled towels and pillows were placed to support the injured woman's wrist and under her knees. During the ride to the hospital, Millie, exhausted from her ordeal, was quiet, in too much pain to talk.

Shay withdrew into her own thoughts. It must be hard growing old alone. Millie had her grandson, but he was the only family member who looked in on and helped her. Such a lonely existence. After splitting from Nick, Shay worried that she too would grow old alone.

When they arrived at the hospital, Millie's grandson stood waiting by the ER entrance. "Nana, the neighbor called me. Are you ok?"

Jen, one of the nurses, came to meet them as they

entered through the sliding glass doors.

The ER hummed with activity. Machines beeped and voices blended in, making a cacophony of noise.

Shay gave Jen the report and transferred Millie's care to her. Knowing the elderly woman was in good hands, she and Joanna waved goodbye. They stopped near the sliding glass doors to the ER. They remade the stretcher, restocked supplies, and then headed to home base.

The sun lit the horizon in pinks and purples, chasing away the dark blue of night. It was almost time for them to turn the keys over to the day shift.

Joanna snored lightly from the passenger side.

Shay yawned. After the long night, she was tired. But it was a good tired, knowing she made a difference in people's lives.

Tall Tales

by

Laura Strickland

"Did I ever tell you 'bout the time I wrestled a crazy Mongolian for some noodles?" Deacon asked. "This was back in the days when hobos used to ride the rails. He and I were sharin' a boxcar, see? And I hadn't eaten in ten days..."

The men gathered inside Nielson's General Store gave a collective groan.

An old building—older even than the wizened gentlemen who now occupied the area around its wood-burning stove—Nielson's had been a mainstay in town since before any of them was born. Except Deacon. He claimed he remembered when the walls of Nielson's went up and had described the building process at length.

Usually, these aging friends met out on the wide planks of the front porch. There, they shared time that tended to hang heavy on their hands since retirement, along with stories and memories. Not today, though, for a cold October rain pounded down outside. Only a fool would walk away from the cozy warmth of Nielson's on such an afternoon, even if staying did mean a man had to listen to Deacon's bullshit.

"And you poked him in the eye and pulled his long, black hair and made him give up them noodles," supplied Wiley Gorman, who didn't think he could endure listening to that same old tale one more time. "And then you shared the noodles with him ..."

"Then I shared them noodles with the man," said Deacon with great dignity, as if he hadn't heard Wiley's interruption. "'Cause I knew what it felt like to be

67

hungry, and you have to leave even a defeated man his pride."

The oldsters—six in number besides Deacon—exchanged dour looks with one another. Not one of them there hadn't heard the "Mongolian" story at least a dozen times. True, it wasn't always the same: sometimes Deacon exaggerated one detail or another, turning the Mongolian into a professional wrestler or the noodles into a tasty can of stew.

Wiley, who'd been the town's grease monkey until he retired, pulled a stogie from his pocket and then put it away again, hastily. They were allowed to smoke out on the porch, but if he lit up in the store, Eric Nielson's wife, Donna, would come down on him like ten exes. Wiley thought about going on home, but the rain drummed on the roof of the store with the intensity of a maniacal rock drummer. He also considered calling Deacon on the veracity of his stories, telling him he was full of hot air, but bit his tongue instead.

"Well then," Deacon started up again, wheezing like a bagpipe, "did I ever tell you 'bout the time Martians landed in the back forty out at Henderson's farm? A clear night it was, and I was walking home after delivering Elmer Wright's kid. Not his blood kid, you understand, but the goat his prize nanny was carrying. She was having trouble giving birth, and Elmer knew what a deft hand I was with small stock. He sent his boy Timmy running to fetch me, and I delivered him a fine, strapping billy goat, too big in the head for his ma to manage alone."

You're big in the head, Wiley thought with a wave of annoyance. Why couldn't the old fella let someone else get a word in edgewise? "Anybody want a game of checkers?" he proposed, hoping to head off the remainder of the Martian story.

"Now hold on, young fellow, you just listen. No need to get all impatient." Deacon broke into a wide grin, which didn't do his face any favors. The man had lost his dentures years ago, and beneath the battered old cap he always wore, he was all gums and wrinkles. "Listen up and you might learn something."

"Huh," said Bert Mathers, a man of few words. He got up, opened the door of the stove, and very deliberately spat inside.

Wiley grinned to himself; it made a valid statement.

"We've heard the Martian story, God damn it," said Mike Evans. "If you're going to take up room next to the stove, at least tell us one we haven't heard."

"Hmm." Deacon breathed and stared at the ceiling as if trying to recall the details of an adventurous past.

Fat chance. Wiley bet the old stoat hadn't done a fraction of the things he claimed.

Eric Nielson, the shopkeeper, idle on this wet afternoon, leaned across his counter and grinned. "He don't have any new stories, boys. You'll just have to listen to the old ones over again"

"Damned if I will," Mike said.

Phil Ellison belched his agreement.

"Just lemme think." Deacon shoved a finger inside his filthy cap and scratched his head. "I'll bet I never told you about the time them bank robbers came through town on their way out of Bowmansville, and old lady Reynolds' dog chased 'em silly."

"Sure, you did." Wiley goaded him. "You told us the dog bit one of 'em in the butt and made him howl like a little girl."

"No," objected Billy, "you said that old dog bit one on the ankle and made him drop part of that gold they stole from the vault."

"Actually—" Eric Nielson added his contribution. "—you told us the dog had 'em cornered and you were the only one who could call the brute off, so you made them give you a cut of the gold before they could get away." He winked at his fellow listeners.

"Yep, that's right." Deacon screwed up his eyes and thought about it. "Old lady Reynolds' dog was called Chase, and damned if that wasn't what he liked to do. That dog would chase a fart if he heard it go by. But he listened to me, cause I used to work on her place." A sly expression came over Deacon's face. "Among other things."

"Ack!" Bert shook his head. "You ain't asking us to believe you and that old stick of a woman ever warmed each other's bones?"

"We were both a lot younger then. And a man's gotta do what a man's gotta do. Doesn't mean I shared the gold with her, though." He shot a look at his listeners. "It's still buried out on her place."

"That's the biggest load of manure I ever heard." Billy smacked his leg. "You mean to tell me you've got a share of gold buried someplace, but you're living in that shack you call home? Pull my other one!"

"What do I want with gold?" Deacon demanded. "I got everything I need: a place to lay my head at night, good friends, and money for beer. Why complicate my life?"

His listeners exchanged glances again.

Wiley thought about unpropping himself from the doorway where he leaned and leaving. Maybe he'd stop

70

by the diner and see if Beth Anne had any pie left. He was just wasting his time here.

"I'll let you boys in on a little secret." Deacon leaned forward in the creaky chair Eric afforded him. "I'm not gonna live forever, you know. Once I'm gone, that gold will be fair game. I planted it under a big old alder tree so it would be easy to find."

"Alder tree?" Jim snorted. "Fat lot of good that will do you, Deak. Old lady Reynolds' whole property's grown up with alders since she stopped farming it."

Wiley shook his head. Had there ever been a bigger bullshitter than old Deacon? Why did he bother listening?

"But you fellows wanted to hear a story I never done told before." Deacon frowned. "Let's see. Did I ever tell you 'bout the time I was in the daredevil act?"

"No," said Eric, no doubt bored with his lack of customers and willing to be amused. "When was this?"

"Had to be thirty years ago. Lots of traveling shows used to come through here back then—hawkers and even a circus, once."

"Sure, I remember the circus," Jim put in. "They had that elephant that ran amok and crushed Jed Hoffelt's car. People came from miles around after, to look at it."

"Well—" Deacon took up the tale. "—the one time it was this troop of daredevils. They had them a cannon and a fellow with no arms who they shot out of it. Damnedest thing you ever saw. When he landed, he rolled over and over like a human cannonball until he came to rest, all covered with smudges and soot."

Wiley narrowed his eyes. This story almost sounded legitimate. *Almost.*

"Yeah?" Eric Nielsen encouraged. "What else?"

"Well now, let me see if I can remember. They had a fellow—big, hairy brute—who was willing to take on all comers with his fists. And another who threw axes and knives, all at the same time. They had a lady who swallowed fire." He paused reflectively. "Made a man wonder what else she might be able to swallow, I can tell you that."

"Whoo-hoo!" Several of the men hooted.

Even Wiley grinned reluctantly.

"And—" Deacon pressed on. "—they had this fellow, an archer, who claimed he could shoot anything clean off of anywhere."

"Oh, yeah, 'cause there's a lot of master archers wandering the cornfields in these parts," Bert jeered.

"This one said he could nail a fly at fifty paces." Deacon insisted. "And you could challenge him, like. If you put down a quarter, you could ask him to target whatever you wanted. A quarter was a lot of money in them days. But if he missed, you won the whole pot."

"So, did he ever miss?" Wiley was interested in spite of himself.

"He did not. I tell you, nothing ruffled that fellow. I saw him shoot a cigarette out of a pretty girl's mouth, saw him shoot a bone off a dog's nose. I even saw him flick a match out of the Sheriff's hand. But me, I thought I'd be able to challenge him and take that pot."

"'Course you did," Jim grumbled. "Cause you're always thinkin', right Deak?"

"I had me a gumdrop in my pocket. It'd been there since Easter, see, and it must have been June when this took place. I laid down my quarter—spent three days earning that, mind—and plopped that gumdrop on top of my head, thinkin', *all right, you smarmy customer, let's see what you can do!*"

This, Wiley did not believe. Nobody, not even this old coot, could be that stupid.

"Well, when it was my turn, I stood up there, straight and tall, with that gumdrop on my head. With a smirk the archer drew his bow. I saw that arrow comin' for me, and boys, it looked like it was gonna take me plumb between the eyes. I kinda ducked and that damn arrow parted my hair, and took that gumdrop clean off my head."

Dead silence met this pronouncement.

It got so quiet in the store, Wiley could hear the fire popping and the rain pounding the roof.

Then Bert said roundly, "Bullshit! You've told us a load of tall tales in your time, old man, but only an idiot would believe that. Who'd be fool enough to let a man fire an arrow at his head?"

"It's true!" Deacon asserted. "If I'd been any taller, boys, I wouldn't be here talking to you now."

General laughter ensued, most of it good-humored.

But Wiley leaned toward the old man and said, "You know, Deak, I don't appreciate bein' lied to."

"Who's lyin'?" The old man's rheumy eyes widened in a parody of innocence. "Every story I ever done told you fellows is true. And I can prove it."

Before anybody could speak, the old man leaned forward in his chair and swept the dirty cap from his head.

Wiley didn't suppose he'd ever seen Deacon without that cap before, and now he figured why. Deacon must have gone bald some time ago, and his pale scalp shone in the store lamps—except for the furrowed scar that parted it, front to back, the whole length of his head.

"There's the mark that arrow left!" Deacon cried

victoriously.

A second silence fell, this one far deeper than the first. It was broken when someone cleared his throat.

"Sorry we doubted you, Deak," Bert muttered.

"Yeah, sorry. Good story." Wiley thought hard for a minute. "Say, Eric, you got any of them shovels left, the ones you were selling last week at half price?"

"Well, sure," Eric said, "but they're back up to full price this week."

"Go get me one anyway. I got a mind to do some digging in those flower beds out back of my house."

"And I've been meaning to move my outhouse," Jim said quickly. "You fetch me one of them shovels too, Eric, hear?"

"Yep," Bert drawled, "my wife's been after me to dig out that wild rosebush." He paused and listened to the rain. "You say you planted that gold of yours under an alder tree, Deak?"

"Out at Mrs. Reynolds'. But hey, where are all you fellows going? Wouldn't you rather stay here out of the rain?"

"Gotta go," they said one by one as they handed over their money and purchased their shovels from Eric.

Last to leave, about to go out into the driving rain, Wiley turned back in hopes old Deacon might tell him something more. What he needed was a hint that would help him get ahead of all the other geezers on their way out to the Reynolds' place.

He was just in time to see Deacon and Eric Nielsen exchange a nod and a wink as Eric placed a cut of the shovel sales' money into the old man's hands. Smiling ruefully, Wiley went out into the rain. Maybe he'd just stop by the diner and get that pie after all.

Fare Gain

by

Alexandra Christle

The massive house, nestled along the Virginia Beach oceanfront, loomed above the circular driveway. Mick O'Reilly pulled his taxicab up near the door and waited for the man to gather his things. Reflected in the review mirror, the guy ran his hand over the seat, patted his pockets, then shrugged and reached inside his jacket, pulling out some cash.

"Here shya go, buddy." He shoved the crumpled bills Mick's way, pushed open the car door, and crawled from the back seat, dragging his tote behind him.

Mick thrust some change through his open window, but the guy waved it off, slapping the cab's roof before heading up the walk, his gait slow and unsteady. "Tanks, pal," his slightly slurred words drifted through the motionless, warm night air.

Responding with a nod of acknowledgement, Mick blew out a breath and let his head drop against the headrest. The guy was nice enough, but drunk and chatty as hell, and at eleven p.m., the last thing Mick wanted was conversation. Somehow, his fare had gotten Mick to spill his guts about his grandson. Little Mickey, the light of his life who wouldn't live to see his tenth birthday.

The dismal thought dropped over Mick like a heavy plastic tarp, and he brushed his shoulder in an effort to shake it off. He pulled around the drive and headed to Norfolk. Time to turn in the car and beat feet to his shabby three-room apartment above the health-food restaurant.

Mick made the long haul back from the beach in record time, cruising down I-264 doing seventy-five miles per hour—this late on a weeknight, traffic was light.

Exiting the interstate, he steered the bright green and white painted car through the deserted side streets to the garage. It always gave him the creeps when he took this shift, but he'd learned the hard way. If he took the company car home, someone would flag him down for a ride—it never failed. Mick found an empty space near his aging mustard-brown Corolla, shut off the cab's engine, and gathered up his paperwork and belongings. After clearing the front out, he opened the back door to make sure no trash had been dumped on the floor. His gaze fell on something square and brown.

Someone had dropped their freaking wallet.

Aw, hell. Why tonight? His whole body had been aching all damn day, and all he wanted was to go home, pop open a beer, stand under the shower for a few minutes, and then hit the sack. His back spasmed as he bent over to scoop up the offending article. Slowly, he straightened, his grip tight on the bulging billfold. His muscles twinged again before he could stand fully upright. He never should've jumped in the middle of that group of kids playing basketball in The Plot in Norfolk's NEON District yesterday afternoon.

Kids. Yeah. Those twenty-somethings were in good shape. At least he'd made a long-shot three-pointer. It almost made the pain worth his effort.

Mick raised his shoulders and rolled his head, making his bones crackle. The wallet flopped open, and the picture of his last fare stared up from the driver's license under the clear plastic slot—*Richard L. Masten.*

Judging by its thickness, the wallet must have a couple dozen credit cards in the thing. The man told Mick during the ride he'd lost a bundle in Vegas over the weekend, so it couldn't be cash. A deep sigh swirled from Mick's mouth, and he peered into the bill section.

He quickly froze, only able to blink.

The wallet was stuffed, and not with credit cards. No bills smaller than a hundred, a few thousands...*they don't even make those anymore. Where the hell did he get them?* Mick rifled through the greenbacks, his heart pounding.

Ten thousand dollars.

Ten. Thousand.

Almost four months' income for him. Right here, in his hand. He sagged against the door, staring at the wad of cash.

"Yo, Mick! Have a good night?" Another driver crossed the lot toward his car.

He stuffed the wallet in his pocket. "Decent enough. Got a pretty good tip from my last fare." *Pretty good. Ha.*

Mick limped over to his Corolla and slid onto the seat, then pulled the billfold out of his pocket to stare at it some more. He could take this money and help his daughter pay some of little Mickey's medical bills. Maybe get him more treatments and buy him some time.

A smile crossed his face as an image of a teenaged Mickey, playing baseball, wrapped around his heart. Then the picture disappeared.

What're you thinking? The guy had paid him, so he'd know it was the last place he'd had his wallet. He stared out the windshield. A light breeze ruffled the leaves in the surrounding trees, the bright moon turning them a shadowy silver-gray. His mind flashed over the scene. Masten hadn't pulled out his wallet—it looked like he'd rummaged for it, then reached in his jacket pocket and handed Mick the cash.

He might think he'd lost it at the airport. Or maybe on the plane.

If the guy called the office and asked, Jennie, the dispatcher, would tell him no wallets had been turned in. She'd track it back to Mick, but he'd deny any knowledge of the man's belongings. Masten might be suspicious, but what could he do? And Jennie would back him up—everyone in the company knew Mick was honest to a fault.

Maybe not as much as they thought.

He raked his fingers through his hair, stopping to massage his neck. Virtue versus vice. Morality versus sin. Unbidden, an image of Sister Anna's tall figure loomed before him. Her withering glare making him cringe as he slouched at the front of the Catholic school's classroom.

Michael O'Reilly. You will be punished for this. Return this money, tonight.

A grimace crept across his face. The nun was dead, and still she hovered in his mind, slapping the wooden ruler against her palm. Right before she was about to whack him across the backside. Even in the afterlife, she wielded a heavy hand.

Eyes closed, he dropped his head. For several minutes, he sat in a mental purgatory.

A deep, elongated sigh oozed from his chest, like sap from a bleeding maple. Slow, sticky, choking his air. He drew in a strained breath and started the car—the *rannt-rannt-rannt* of the dying battery groaning in the darkness. Finally, it caught and roared to a sputtering start.

The lot's gate creaked open, agonizingly slow. *Hurry the hell up.* Mick needed that shower and beer. And time to think. His vehicle chugged from the parking area. Along the empty Norfolk streets, oak tree canopies lined the sides, shrouding them in dancing shadows. A lone set of headlights came toward him, then passed, both of their vehicles nameless, invisible, anonymous in the late night hours.

Thoughts of the money in his pocket continued to prick the hairs at the back of his neck, giving him a chill. He turned the corner by his apartment and parked on a side street. At least once a month, a car parked out front would get smashed by some drunk driver, heading away from downtown, so Mick avoided those spaces.

Car locked, he trudged past the new nightclub, nodding at the muscled, dark-skinned security guard out front. A dozen people sat inside, at the bar and tables. Quiet night.

After unlocking the door to the stairwell, he plodded his way up, bones popping with every step, left hand bracing his hip as he used the handrail to take some pressure off his knees and back.

"*Mmph.*" With one final pull, he landed at his door, unlocked it, and pushed inside, heading straight for the fridge. Two cans of Miller High Life nestled in the rack. He grabbed one. *High Life. Right.* Dropping into his easy chair, he rolled the can over his forehead then drew his cool damp hand across the back of his neck as he pulled the tab and took a long draw of the beer.

With each swallow, he sank further into the cushions, mulling over his choices. Sister Anna poked at his brain like Billy Walters used to do to with his chubby fingers, shoving at Mick's chest when they were ten.

Damn bully.

He blew out a hard breath. Ten. The age his grandson wouldn't see. He squeezed his eyes against threatening tears then plunked the can on the side table and shoved away from the chair. He grabbed his keys and headed out.

****

For the second time tonight, Mick pulled his car into the drive and studied the massive house. From the looks of this place, the guy may have lost a bundle in Vegas, but he had a bundle he could lose. Maybe he *should* take the money and split. No one would ever know.

Sister Anna's voice teased the edges of his thoughts. Again, he heard the ruler slapping his behind as his classmates watched in fear. Billy Walters snickered—until she grabbed him up, too.

Muttered curses slipped from Mick's mouth as he crawled from the car and trudged to the huge front door. Almost midnight, but lights shone through the windows. Someone was still awake. He drew up his shoulders and rang the bell. A deep Westminster chime echoed behind the oversized wooden door before a voice came through a hidden intercom.

"Jah. Who goes 'ere?" the voice slurred.

He bent over the small speaker mounted by the door. "Uhh, Mick O'Reilly… I gave you a lift—"

A buzzer sounded at the same time the guy's voice boomed out of the box. "My taxshi guy!"

Mick jerked back at the sudden overloud response.

"Come on in, come on in. Head straight downa hall to the back of the house."

A grimace knotted his cheek muscles, and he wasted

no time twisting the doorknob, more to stop the incessant whining buzz of the locking mechanism than to actually go inside. He stepped across the threshold and pulled the door closed, and his eyebrows shot up.

Holy bejesus, he could've walked into the Smithsonian and not seen this much…stuff. The middle of the entrance hall held an antique round table with a ginormous display of fresh flowers. Rooms that were open on either side of the hall had walls covered with huge paintings and some kind of abstract sculptures. He didn't even know what half of this crap was.

"Whew." His gaze darting around the long hall, Mick trekked along the white marble floor, his footsteps silent on the padded, thick Oriental rug extending the length of the corridor. After what seemed like a five-minute hike through a museum, he landed in front of open double-doors, and a voice called out.

"C-come on in, Mick, my friend. Have a drink."

His fare lounged in an oversized, overstuffed rocker, feet propped on a matching ottoman. One corduroy loafer hung from his big toe, the other rested on the floor. Mick's host lifted a cut crystal rocks glass, swirled the amber liquid, and pointed to a wet bar. "Open that cabinet and have whatever sha want, buddy."

If the next word out of this character's mouth was *pal*, he'd be tempted to slug him. But Masten only watched in silence while Mick scanned the rows and pulled out a bottle of Glenfiddich single malt. Why the hell not? Buying himself a bottle of Johnnie Walker Red every Christmas was his one treat for the year. He nursed that bottle until March.

When he'd poured three fingers and dropped in an ice cube from the silver bucket, he turned, and Masten motioned him toward a chair. "Ya got good taste in booze, buddy." He took more than a sip from his glass then set it on his leg, his gaze riveted on Mick the entire time.

Mick tried not to stare at the man, but from the corner of his vision as he glanced around the room he could see Masten tremble. His hand shook each time he took a swallow of his drink, and when Mick stole another look, a few drops dribbled from the guy's mouth onto his shirt. He'd had more than enough to drink, it appeared.

Small talk didn't seem to be in the cards, so Mick sat, sipping on the scotch, letting it roll over his tongue before it slid down his throat like warm silk. Maybe the guy was just lonely, wife out of town, who knew? If he needed some company while he got himself even more sloshed, Mick could live with that—for a short time anyway.

After a couple of minutes, Masten rose, straggled to the bar, and got a glass of ice water. He then turned and leaned against the granite countertop. From behind the rim of the glass nearing his lips, he said, "You found my wallet."

Mick jerked and tried not to spit out the scotch in his mouth. With a slight cough, he set the glass on a table. "Uh, yessir, I did."

Masten nodded, but it was more like a twitch. His movements jerky and spastic. "Knew you were an honest guy. I figured you'd shup…" he stuttered and tried again. "Show up ch-chamorrow, though. Kinda late to come now."

What was this guy's deal? Mick shifted in the chair and started to pull out the billfold from his pocket, but the man held up his hand to stop him.

"Don't want it. I could use my driver's license back, but the money's yours." He drained the water.

"Mr. Mast—"

"Call me Rich, Mick." He laughed and jerked his arm through the air, encompassing the room. "Rich. Get it?" He laughed again, too hard and too loud, shoulders lurching.

Mick needed to get out of here. Something about this guy wasn't right.

"Got more money than I can spend in my lifetime." With that declaration, his face fell, a morose expression settling in his eyes and on his mouth.

The depth of sadness consuming the man had Mick repositioning himself and swallowing more of the scotch to hide his reaction. Whatever was eating at this guy was digging deep. Mick had been driving a taxi for thirty years. It was like being a bartender. People told him all kinds of crap, assuming their confessions were anonymous and they'd never see him again.

He'd heard some doozies and gotten pretty good at reading people.

Rich stared at the floor, then said, "I need your help, Mick." He looked up. "You're an honesht guy, and I'll pay you well. The ten grand is just a deposit, but whether you help me or not, I don't want the money back." His gaze drifted to something behind Mick. "Can't use it where I'm going."

Mick stood and set the billfold on the table. "Look, Mr. Masten…"

"Risch."

"Mr. Masten." This guy wasn't a friend of his, and keeping this formal seemed the better option. "I can't take your money. It's a hell of a nice offer, but—"

"Go a long way with that grandson of yoursh." He moved back to his chair and plopped heavily into the seat. "Jush hear me out."

The silence in the room wrapped around them, pressing against Mick. An ice cube shifted with a *clink* in the glass Rich had left on the sidebar, the only other sound in the room a faint *tick-tick-tick* from a grandfather clock in the corner. Masten contorted his body, a wince skirting his face as he opened a drawer and pulled out a plastic zipper bag with two hypodermic needles.

A chill stung Mick's neck, crawled over his shoulders, and crept down his spine.

The hand that held the pouch shook, but more like a vibration than a tremor. Rich let out a weak cough and watched Mick for several eternal seconds, then swallowed so hard the gulp echoed from his throat.

"I need for you to help me die."

****

Mick collapsed against the chair's back, his gaze on the man.

Rich kept his gaze steady, even with the slight spasms in his body. "Why don't you refill your glassh, buddy? Hate to see that bottle go to waste. In fact, take it with you. Take the whole damn bar."

Mick couldn't move, could do nothing but continue to peer at him, blinking. Sister Anna blasted recriminations in his head, but her sermons weren't needed. He had enough objections of his own.

When Mick remained speechless, Masten continued, speaking slowly, making a visible effort to enunciate clearly. "I don't have anyone, Mick. My wife and daughter…" he paused, grief etching his features, "…died in a car accident twenty years ago. I didn't…couldn't…remarry. I just worked. Worked my assh off. Made a sinful amount of money." He squeezed his eyes briefly then blinked rapidly. "No one to share it with." His head drooped forward, and he stopped speaking for several seconds.

The silence in the room began to squeeze at Mick's temples, making his head throb. He ran a hand across his forehead. "Mr… Rich, I don't know what you have in mind, but I can't—"

Rich held up a shaking hand. "You help me, and I'll make sure that little grandson of yours gets that treatment he needs." He blinked again. "Kids deserve a chance to live."

Mick's throat closed up. The new treatment that would save Mickey's life cost hundreds of thousands of dollars. Insurance wouldn't pay for the procedure and medications. They'd gone through every avenue they could find and still came up short. Yet… He couldn't take someone else's life, not even to save another's.

Rich seemed to read his thoughts. "You mishunderstand. I—I got this. Not asking you to…pull the trigger. Got this needle. I can do it myself. Takes about twenty minutes, I've been told." He paused. "I got no one, Mick. I don't…" His voice lowered, forcing Mick to strain to hear him. "Been alone for twenty years. I don't want to die alone."

Mick swallowed hard as a hand gripped his heart and squeezed. He didn't know this guy from Adam, but his plea drove straight into his heart. Wrenched it from his chest.

"Look, Rich, I…I… Are you sure you want to do this? What are you, about my age? Fifty? Whatever's wrong, you can get some help—"

Rich spat out a hard, grunted laugh. "Not for this. I've got ALS. Gonna die anyway, and I don't want to go through the suffering. Rather do it while I'm shtill... still got..." He closed his eyes.

Images flashed through Mick's mind, and he frowned. "That's... Lou Gehrig's Disease? But people can live for years... Stephen Hawking lived fifty—"

"Hawking was an ab-abbera... fluke." The thickness in Rich's speech choked the air. "Not sitting around with a feeding tube and wires in my brain so I can c-communicate. Already having problems... I'm not drunk. Jusht can't talk." A deep sigh came from his chest. "I wasn't in Vegas gamblin'. Had to get this stuff"—he tipped his head toward the needles—"out there. Can't around here." He shifted in the chair and leaned up. "I've got all my affairs set up. My lawyer knows. Gotta call him, and he'll come over when I'm... it's done."

The desperation in Rich's tone, on his face... but why Mick? Why now? "Can't you just have him—"

"Won't do it. Known him for years. Says he can't."

Tension pulled at Mick's facial muscles. "But you think I can? I don't even know—"

Rich's eyes pleaded with him. "That ten grand won't even cover one treatment for your grandson. You sit with me. That's it. Just sit with me. And the kid gets a chance."

Dear God. A long breath escaped Mick's chest. How could he say no?

How could he say yes?

He shook his head, the moral dilemma cruising through his brain. Sitting with the guy wouldn't be illegal. But letting him take his own life, watching it, not intervening… could he do that? *What do you have to say about that, Sister?*

The nun had no response.

Masten shoved forward in the chair and struggled to rise. Mick jumped up to help him, but he shook his head. "Why doncha go out by the pool? Gotta call my attorney and then I'll come out there. Get yourself a drink." He moved toward some French doors and opened them for Mick.

With seemingly no option but to follow the man's orders, Mick splashed some scotch in his glass and wandered outside, dropping onto a thick cushioned wicker chair. Over the ocean, the moon rode high in the clear sky, reflecting off the white crests of the lapping waves. He waited—for what, he couldn't say. Ten, twenty minutes, an hour… *Death?* How did he manage to get himself into this mess?

And yet, this *mess* would save his grandson's life. Mick would give his own life in a heartbeat to save the boy, but for a stranger? A scuffing pulled him from his thoughts as Rich shuffled outside.

The two men sat, next to one another, in silence until Rich began to talk. A mission, a confession, a life story—it unraveled while Mick stayed nearly motionless, mesmerized by the man's history, until a soft glow tinted the edge of the horizon.

"And now here I sit with you," Rich brought his monologue to a close. "I'm ready now."

Mick started—he'd all but forgotten why he sat here with this man. A gentleman who'd had a productive and impactful life, tainted with an emptiness Mick couldn't fathom. Thick scattered clouds in the east reflected the sun in bright hues of a pink and gold sunrise.

"That's what I wanted to see, one more time," Rich said. He drew the plastic bag from his pocket and peeled it open, pulling out a damp cotton ball and one needle. "This one's shposed to make me relax… I might drift off. Don't know." He chuckled. "Never done this before."

"Rich—"

"Don't, Mick." Hand trembling, he rolled up his sleeve and rubbed the cotton over his arm, an ironic smirk on his face. "Don't want to get an infection." He snapped the cap off the needle, paused for only a second, tapped and jabbed it into his upper arm. "Addison, my lawyer, will be here in about an hour. You can wait for him if you want, but if ya wanna leave, he knows how to find you." He waited for a few minutes then said, "Guess I'd better finish this up before I fall asleep." He rummaged for the other hypodermic, repeated his actions, shot one more look at the sunrise, and plunged the needle in his arm.

Mick reached over and laid his hand on Rich's forearm.

He grabbed Mick's hand in a tight grip. "Thank you."

Quiet, incessant ticks from the grandfather clock filtered through the patio doors, puncturing the still morning air. No one spoke. They stayed in that position, Mick clamping down his hold as Rich's grasp loosened.

"This isn't so bad. Nice… No pain," Rich mumbled and closed his eyes. Time crawled, time raced. Then his chest stopped moving.

A tightness gripped at Mick's throat, and he struggled to swallow. A life given for a life gained. The rising sun burned through his skin, searing his heart.

Michael O'Reilly closed his eyes and wept.

The Note

by

Stephen B. King

I very nearly didn't see the note as it lay on the wet ground, forlornly. Its bent over corner was dipped in a puddle, which reminded me of a soggy corn chip in salsa. The rain had caused the water to travel up the paper, slowly spreading the written letters that were face-down on the concrete so they looked *fluffy*.

Sometimes, when I am having one of my darker moods, I wish I'd stepped over it and kept walking. But at other times, I comfort myself knowing had I done that, I could never have saved Simone Brereton's life. On my better days, it's a close-run race between regret and feeling glad to have been there to help. As it turned out, it cost me the use of my legs. Was that a fair trade? You be the judge.

I suppose the weirdest thing about the whole episode is that the writing on the note was underneath as it lay on the ground. Had it not been raining, and the ink starting to bloom like the petals of a chrysanthemum, the word HELP would not have bled through to have been visible. Also, if the weather had been dry, the wind could have carried it away, to land somewhere else, and Simone could have died.

The note, at first glance, looked like it had been ripped unceremoniously from a spiral note pad and had the look of being crumpled up and discarded. The elements had allowed it to open, and the rain stuck it to the pavement. That one word, HELP, was diagonally written in big scrawly letters and the P was closest to the corner hanging in the puddle. As it soaked up the water, much as a sponge would, it made the ink visible. It was that phenomena which made it readable from the reverse side as I hurried from my car to get to the front door of my house.

So if it hadn't been for an accumulation of odd coincidences, I wouldn't have stopped mid-stride, made sure I saw the word in backward writing, and then stooped to pick it up. While I'm speaking about weird coincidences, there was another. If I had not felt the stirrings of an approaching migraine, I wouldn't have left the office early. Then, even if I had found the note later, the rain would have washed the ink away, and there would have been nothing left to see.

From years of headache experience, I knew the signs well. Within two hours, I would be in so much pain I wouldn't be able to see clearly. Going home while I was still able to drive was vital, so I turned off my computer, told my assistant Jane I was leaving for the day, and left. That's the benefit of owning my own business. Isn't life bizarre sometimes, though? With what later transpired, the migraine didn't appear at all. And what I find interesting about that is they tell me they are brought on by stress. Well, looking at numbers on a computer was nowhere near as stressful as what was about to unfold.

It's hard to describe my emotions as I stood, with the rain beating down, looking stupidly at the word HELP, and trying to make sense of it. I had not taken an overcoat or umbrella to work with me earlier in the day because it was a quite typically warm late spring day when I left the house that morning.

I remembered a practical joke we used to play on passers-by when I was a youth, and quickly looked around for any giggling children who could be watching. In my day, we used to take delight in using Super Glue to cement a gold coin to the pavement, and then laugh uproariously as some schmuck would attempt to pick it up. Was this a trick in a similar vein, I wondered? There was no one else I could see hiding anywhere, which discounted that theory. As you'd expect, on such a wet day, Tippington Close was devoid of anyone, other than me.

My searching eyes returned to the paper, then darted straight back up to something my peripheral vision had picked up on. *Why is Derek and Simone's bedroom window open when it's raining?*

Another thought followed that one: if the note had been thrown away to be found, as opposed to being dropped from a pocket, it made sense it had to have come from a window. I looked up and down the street again and realized two things. Firstly, there were no other windows open I could see, and secondly, while it belted down with rain, there was no wind, not even a breeze. Ergo, the note could not have traveled too far, and that took my eyes straight back to the open window. I had a further realization then. I had noticed, and then overlooked, a car, parked somewhat haphazardly against the curb outside their home, and it looked very out of place.

Mount Lawley, where I live, is a lovely area. Not the best suburb in Perth, you understand, but far from the worst. Tippington Close contained precisely thirteen houses, and we all knew each other. One thing I can tell you is that no one living here owned the old dark blue Ford Falcon sedan, currently sitting outside number seven.

I'm sure you've heard the expression, the hackles on the back of your neck? Well, mine rose right then, and for good measure, goosebumps rose along my arms inside my shirt. Somehow, and I know this will be hard to understand, I just knew Simone was in trouble inside. Hot on the heels of that idea, or call it a premonition if you will, I had another. If she was in trouble, whoever gave her such grief causing her to throw a plea for help into the rain, could be watching me through a window.

Exaggeratedly, in case I had an audience, I shook my head and carried on to my house. I put my key in the slot of the front door, with trembling fingers that didn't want to work, and twisted it. Once opened, I walked inside, firmly closing the oak door behind me, and felt an immediate sense of relief. I leaned against the wall, trying to slow my beating heart and make sense of the washing machine tumbling action of thoughts racing around in my brain.

Had I imagined things? Possibly, I had to concede. The note could be a prank from a kid, and Simone could be out at the shops, having opened the window when the weather was warm and pleasant earlier in the day. *Could it be that simple, and I have imagined the rest? Yes, but what about the car?* I asked myself in response. *Well, it could belong to a tradesman who is working in one of the homes in the street,* I supposed. But, in my heart and soul, I knew that was not the case. Don't ask me how, I just knew, okay?

So what to do, I wondered. My initial idea was to phone the police. *Don't be a bloody idiot,* my alter ego answered. *Seriously, what would I say?* They would think it was Looney Tunes Hour, and even if they thought the note was real, there was no way of knowing it came from my neighbor's window. Meanwhile, if something nasty was going on inside, precious hours could be lost trying to get help when I was right there.

Okay, I know what you are thinking, what am I, The Batman in disguise? An ex highly trained soldier, a retired cop? Nope, I'm a chartered accountant whose wife was away in Darwin visiting her sister, who had been diagnosed with stage three cancer. So I'm just an average guy who had never been in a fight at school or rescued a damsel in distress. I don't get to meet very many damsels in Mount Lawley.

But something was going on next door, I knew it in my bones, and I had to go and investigate. Had I not, and something dreadful happened, I would never have been able to live with myself. I crossed to the closet in the hallway, stripped off my wringing wet suit jacket, and took out a lightweight waterproof one. I kicked off my shoes and crammed my feet into my gardening sneakers.

The next stop was the kitchen, where above the butcher's block food preparation area was the knife rack. I slid out a twelve-inch Japanese beauty that was as sharp as my mother-in-law's tongue. Then, holding the knife as if it were a weapon, I got a fit of the giggles. *Who am I kidding?* I put the knife back. There is no way I was capable of stabbing someone, no matter what the justification was. I'm more likely to cut myself in the event of a scuffle.

I was halfway across the room when I had an alternate idea which, I decided, was a fair compromise. I hurried to the five-drawer unit and opened the third one down. Amongst all the clutter, I found what I was looking for, my Swiss Army pocket knife, and I tucked it into my jacket. Somehow, I felt better about myself, though part of me thought it was a stupid idea, laughable even, but none the less, it also felt somehow right.

My patio glass sliding door opened out to the rear garden to an area obscured from Simone's house, just in case they were watching. I say they, which I now know to be accurate, but then it was an ethereal *'they.'* For all I knew, *'they'* only existed in my imagination.

Between our two houses was a six-foot-high fence made of bond steel sheets in a cream colour. On either side were trees, plants, and flower beds. Both wives were keen gardeners, so the gardens were full of flowering shrubs. Under normal circumstances, going from one property to the other would not be possible without scaling the wall, which wasn't going to happen, as I would be seen and heard clearly, climbing over a metal fence. We had been friends with our neighbors for many years, and we frequently had each other over for barbeques. So about three years before, a sudden storm blew part of the fence down, and we replaced it via an insurance claim. Derek and I combined to offer the installer a couple of cartons of beer to put in a semi-concealed gate. When Grace, our daughter, got married, we held the reception in our garden inside a marquee, and we propped the gate open so we could utilize both kitchens, bathrooms, and toilets, which was fantastic.

As quietly as possible, I opened it, hoping and praying the hinges hadn't become rusty and would squeak, but my luck was in. I stepped through the opening, closed it behind me and stood in their garden, behind a conifer tree. I listened for any sign I'd been spotted, but there was nothing but the sound of raindrops hitting me after pinballing through the branches of the tree above me.

Then, from inside the house, I heard the unmistakable clattering noise of a piece of cutlery being dropped into a stainless-steel sink, and I let out a sigh of relief. I'd worried about nothing; Simone was home and had just forgotten the window was open. Shaking my head in relief, I left the cover of the tree and crossed the flower bed on the gravel path, and stepped onto the lawn. From there, I crossed to the rear door, which entered their pantry on the side of the kitchen. I opened the door, stepped inside, calling out as I did, "Hey Simone, it's only me. You've left your bedroom window open, and it's raining, you silly goose."

I turned into the kitchen, and my heart sank. Two men stood with open mouths, staring at me as if they had seen a ghost. The second thing I saw lay on the kitchen bench—it was a gun. A big, horrible-looking handgun with what looked like a massive opening in the business end. How huge? Well, I'd never seen anything to compare it to, then one of them picked it up and pointed it squarely at my chest.

"Who are you, mate?" the one with short, spiky, dyed blond hair said. He looked mean, even though he wasn't the one with the pistol. He wore a denim jacket which looked like it hadn't been washed in years, a black T-shirt, and faded jeans.

The taller one had dark curly hair, and part of his right ear was missing as if it had been bitten off in a fight. The other ear had a large, thick, gold earring hanging from it. He, too, wore jeans with a T-shirt, this time a grubby shade of what was once white. His jacket was made of leather and was well-worn. But the thing I noticed most about him was his eyes; they were like looking at two lumps of coal, and by that, I mean dead.

"I'm a neighbor, friends with Simone and Derek. Where is Simone?" I asked as I raised my hands. I couldn't believe how shaky my voice sounded even to me, and I had never been more scared.

"See this 'ere, mate?" the one holding the gun asked. "Imagine if I pulled the trigger right now. It would make an entry hole in your chest oh, say about half an inch in diameter, but, now 'ere's the interesting bit. The exit hole out of your back would be about the size of my fist. So 'ere's the thing, mate—when we ask the questions, it does not give you the right to bloody ask one back. Do you get me?"

I nodded frantically, incapable of speech. If I said I could almost, but thank God not quite, pee in my pants, would you understand I am not kidding? These men were criminals, clearly, and you didn't need to be Sherlock Holmes to figure out they were dangerous. Worse, I thought they would shoot me and not lose one moment of sleep. I was petrified, pure and simple, and thought I was about to be murdered.

"What are we gonna do with him?" Blondie asked his mate.

Here it comes, he's going to shoot me. Then he cocked the hammer back, and I heard the double click as it locked into place. I very nearly fainted as the seconds seemed like hours, time passed in slow motion, and I had the saddest thought about my wife: *I'm not going to be able to say goodbye to Mina.*

"If you want to live, mate, tell me the truth. Is anyone else at home and likely to wander over in the next couple of hours looking for you?"

I shook my head, still not willing to trust my voice. Then Blondie sealed my death warrant when he said,

"He's lying, mate. This job's gone pear-shaped. Kill him and the bitch, and let's get out of here."

Fortunately, right then, I found I could speak; in fact, I found I could beg. "I'm not lying. My wife is in Darwin—her sister just got diagnosed with cancer. I swear I am on my own in the house. I came home early from work, saw Simone's window had been left open, and with it raining, I popped over to tell her. Please don't kill me."

The silence dragged on and on while Curly thought about it, and Blondie fidgeted on first one leg and then the other. After what felt like an hour, Curly released the hammer of the pistol and lowered it.

"It's your lucky day, mate. Let's take him upstairs, tie him up on the bed with the bitch. The husband will be home before five with the money, and then we're out of here. He's agreed to pay up, and I'm not leaving without it."

It occurred to me what they were doing there, in a flash of blinding inspiration. Derek was the manager at the Leederville branch of The Farmers Union Bank, and the men must have broken in and attacked Simone. Somehow she threw the note out of the window, for someone, anyone, to find. Then I guess they phoned Derek and threatened to kill his wife if he did not bring money from the bank vault home with him for her freedom and life. I also realized one more sad fact. They had not worn masks so I could identify them, and I had no doubt when Derek did hand over the money, the three of us would be murdered.

He beckoned with the gun, and like a lamb to the slaughter, hands still held high, and on legs made of jelly, I walked ahead of them to the stairs and climbed on rubbery legs. How I got to the bedroom door on the second floor without stumbling or falling and begging for my life, I will never know. I don't want you to think I was anything other than scared out of my wits; I'm not some super brave guy, I'm Joe average.

Blondie kicked the door ahead of me open, and I saw Simone staring frantically up from the king-sized bed with a rumpled-up quilt cover, where she lay on her back. She had been trussed like a chicken and had a strip of black tape stuck across her mouth. Alarmingly, I noticed the black eye she had and the bloodstains on the side of her face from her broken nose. The blood was smeared by her tears, making the pillow, which was ordinarily white, now pink.

"Look in the wardrobe, get some stuff to tie him up with," Curly said to his mate, before adding, "Looks like it's your lucky day, too, Darlin'," we were all set to have a bit of fun with you before hubby brings the dosh home, but your neighbor here thought he would crash the party."

The next thing I felt was his hand in my back as he shoved me violently forward, so my knees hit the bed and I toppled over to land across it; my upper chest landed on top of Simone's tummy. He dropped his knee onto my backside, brutally, to hold me still as first my left, then right hands were yanked down behind my back, and I felt something soft, like a dressing gown belt, wrapped around and around my wrists and tied off.

Once my feet were secured with one of Derek's leather belts, they shoved me, so I lay alongside Simone on my back. Then from the bedside table, Blondie grabbed a roll of black tape and ripped a good-sized chunk off and stuck across my mouth fiercely, crushing my lips over my teeth as he did.

Curly sat on the edge of the bed and tapped my chest, non-too softly with the tip of the gun barrel. "Listen up, Nosey. We only want the fifty K hubby is going to donate to us when he finishes work, which he agrees is worth it to keep his little lovely here alive. After all, it's not his money, is it? So here's the deal. You two lay here, quiet as little mice, hubby gives us the cash, we bring him up here to join you two, and then we leave. And you all get to play happy families again. But if you make a noise, or piss us off, then we shoot you both and take the money anyway. Are we clear?"

I nodded earnestly, trying with my eyes to convince him I was sincere. They glanced at each other and left, leaving the door wide open as they did, no doubt so they would hear any attempt on our part to escape.

Of course, I struggled to get my hands free of the knotted belt once I heard them walking across the shiny tiled hallway at the bottom of the stairs. Although I could get a few millimeters of play, I wasn't going to get my hands free anytime soon. And worse, the fear and exertion without being able to breathe through my mouth caused my chest to tighten. I felt the early beginnings of an asthma attack coming on. I had no choice but to calm down, try to relax, and get my breathing back under control.

My next idea, unfortunately, enjoyed no better success. I turned my head to Simone and using eye and head gestures, I tried to get her to turn on her side with her back to me. But either she didn't understand what I meant or did but didn't want to risk the two men coming upstairs again to discover us back-to-back trying to undo each other's ropes.

I gave up and worked out how much time we had left on the planet, which sounds all very brave now, but I assure you, I didn't feel it. What I felt was desperation. I knew I left work at around two-forty, so I would have got to my home around three-fifteen. I figured it would now be near three-thirty, and Derek usually got home just after five. I had no idea if he would leave work early with the cash, or he would need to wait until everyone left before stealing it. But one thing I knew about Derek; he would do anything to save Simone, and he would obtain the money to free her. So I realized there could be very little time left before Derek burst in like a knight in armor with a bag full of cash, and we all got shot dead.

At that moment, I had a blinding flash of inspiration. I remembered the Swiss Army knife in my pocket, and with it came a glimmer of hope. But then I wondered how the hell was I going to get it out of my pocket with my hands tied behind my back? I looked down my body at the right-hand jacket pocket where the knife sat positioned in front of my hip. I could feel the weight of it, and when I swizzled my hands out and around to reach it, I came up some four or so inches short no matter how I struggled.

Maybe, I thought, *I can lift my hips while leaving my shoulders on the bed and try to jiggle the damn thing to fall out of my pocket.* Thankfully, I had not done the zipper up, which was there to protect whatever I put inside it from the rain. Lucky really, because usually I am a stickler for doing it up, but on this occasion, having been distracted by my worry for Simone's welfare, it gaped open.

Don't ask me how, but I worked my feet underneath me so I could lift my hips clear of the mattress. Then, using what at any other time might have been quite an obscene motion, I thrust them up and down, and I swear I could feel the knife jiggle around. Out of the corner of my eye, I could see Simone staring at me, petrified the sound of my jerky movements would be heard by the two men downstairs. No doubt had the bed been squeaky they would have, but as befits a bank manager, the bed was excellent quality. Doing what I was doing would only have appeared worse to her because she had no idea I had the means for our escape in my pocket; she probably thought I was going mad.

It took forever, but suddenly I could see the end of the handle poking out of the pocket, and thanking my lucky stars, it took only another minute or so, and it dropped onto the bed, between us.

The asthma had got worse, and breathing through my nose only became more and more difficult. I was also sweating profusely, and a headache approached rapidly, though thankfully not the full-blown migraine, which would have made everything else impossible.

I cannot describe the feeling of joy that washed over me when I wriggled my body upward and around, and I had the knife in my hand. From that point on, it was simple to open the blade, but then it got hard all over again as I hacksawed back and forth over the cloth to try to cut through it. I admit, there were two or three times I thought it impossible, and almost gave up, especially as my wrists were getting slippery with my blood where I kept missing and cutting myself. But never underestimate the extent a man will go to survive. Even if I'd slashed an artery, I think I would have kept cutting.

Well, all I can say is, those Swiss Army guys know their stuff, because eventually, my slippery hands broke free. God, my wrists were a mess. There was blood everywhere, but I didn't feel a thing; adrenaline, I suppose. I sat up and bent forward and freed my legs before turning to Simone, who looked at me with what looked like a mixture of fear and hero worship.

I ripped the tape from my mouth, wincing as I did so. "Shhh, Simone, we have to keep quiet," I whispered after I helped her turn away from me and cut through the rope which bound her. I worried she might have lost the use of her hands because they looked unnaturally blue. Next, I freed her feet and noticed she couldn't use her hands well enough to get a grip on the tape covering her lips, so I helped and, as gently as possible, eased it off.

"What if they come back and find us like this, they will kill us?" she hissed.

"They're going to do that anyway, Simone, they didn't wear masks, and we can identify them. They won't permit it."

She clamped one very blue hand over her open mouth to stifle the gasp as she realized what I said was true.

"How are your hands, and can you walk?"

I watched her try to rub her hands around her wrists to gain some circulation back, and flex her feet. "I can't feel my fingers, but I can walk okay, I think. What shall we do?"

There was the rub, what could we do? I did not doubt that any attempt to go downstairs would be heard, and they would be waiting for us. Then I had an idea. I slipped off the bed and crept around to her side, then helped her stand with one of my hands holding her hand, the other around her waist. She was trembling worse than I was, and believe me, that would have been no mean feat. I gave her a hug for confidence, and she whispered in my ear, "Thank you, thank you so much, George."

These days, when I get depressed about my legs, I remember back to those words, whispered so softly, but so heartfelt, and do you know what? It's not so bad anymore. I put my finger to my lips to remind her to keep quiet, then crossed the room to the window, the one she had left open in the rain, and looked down.

I summed up the situation in an instant and thought, *Yes, it can be done.* I beckoned for Simone to come over, and as she hobbled to me, I had my first doubt. She would be slow, with the loss of circulation to her hands and feet for so long, but that couldn't be helped. I'd have to try to buy her time.

I took my car keys out of my pants pocket, and tucked them into the checked shirt pocket she was wearing, located over her right breast. She looked at me questioningly, so I bent and whispered directly into her ear, "I'm going to lower you out of the window so you can get onto the roof of the dining room below us. I know it's a sloped roof, but from there, you can jump into the flower bed, which with all the rain will be soft. Don't stop, run to my car, jump in and get it started. I'll be right behind you, and if I'm not, if anything goes wrong, drive like the wind and get help. Okay?"

"But they might hear the window open and will be up here in seconds."

"I know, that's why I don't want you to stop for anything. With you gone, Blondie and Curly will know they won't get the money. Derek will be safe, and they'll have no reason to hurt me."

She looked at me with a look akin to love, not that there had ever been anything like that between the four of us, we were just good friends. So far as I could see, it was the only plan which had any chance of success, and in no way made me a hero, it was just about survival. "C'mon, let's do it, we have to get you out of here before Derek gets home."

She nodded, thank goodness. I don't think my nerves could have taken a full-blown discussion. It made sense to get her out, and she had seen the logic. "So once I get the window up all the way, quick as you can, climb out, and let me hold your wrists to lower you down. Don't stop, Simone, not for me or anything—you must get away and get help. Ready?"

She shook her hands one last time to get the blood moving and nodded again. I grabbed the upper sash window and mouthed the words, "*One, two, three.*"

The bloody window screeched all the way up, and we both jumped. Good girl that she was, she flew into action and stuck her left leg through the opening. She grimaced in pain as she gripped the lower sill and swung her other leg through the hole. With a sinking heart, I heard the men running up the stairs.

I grabbed her wrists above the rope marks to help her through and stop her falling because her grip was too weak to support her weight. I braced my knees against the wall below the window and hung on for dear life, then slowly lowered her down, squatting to get her as low as possible.

I let go of Simone's wrists as the men raced into the bedroom. I did the only thing I could think of to do; I stood up to block their view of Simone's escape.

"What the fuck?" It was Curly's voice; they were here.

I stood still and saw Simone jump from the lower

roof into the garden. She landed awkwardly but did not fall, thank God. She turned and looked up at me, and I waved her away, frantically. I had the pleasure of seeing her turn tail and run to my car and get in.

I didn't hear the gunshot, but I felt a kind of a bee sting in the center of my back. My body was thrown forward against the glass, and stupidly, I wondered what the hell had happened. I slowly slid down, dazed and confused, until my top half reached the opening, and I toppled through, into the void, unable to stop myself.

My last waking thought was to wonder why the roof was rushing up to meet me, and meet me it did as I swan-dived onto the tiled surface, made slick with the rain. Mercifully that was when I lost consciousness, so I didn't feel the next drop, from the roof into the garden bed below.

****

When I woke, my wife was holding my hand, and I thought, *But you're in Darwin.* Then I realized I was in a hospital bed. It took time, lots and lots of time to understand what had happened. But then that was one thing I had plenty of.

I'd been in a coma for eleven days. I'd been operated on to remove a bullet from my back where it had lodged against my spine, and a blood clot from my brain. My left arm was broken, and apparently, my face was a mess of healing grazes and bruises.

I'd been awake for three days before they told me I was unlikely ever to walk again. I thought it was because I'd been shot in the back, but no, that hadn't done the damage. It was the landing in the flower bed, half in, and half over the brick retaining wall which held in the mulch.

Luckily, Simone had not seen me fall from the window. If she had, I'm sure she would have stopped to help, and would have been caught by Curly, or Michael Hampton which is his real name, and Blondie, nee Sampson O'Halloran. Simone had driven away in the opposite direction after sideswiping my BMW against the driveway gate in the process.

She quickly found help and sent the police, who responded immediately, and in doing so, probably saved my life. They called the ambulance, and Brad, the paramedic, worked wonders. He recognized the human back was not designed to be in the shape it was, as I lay unconscious in the rain.

Within a day and a half, the two men were apprehended and eventually sentenced to twenty-seven and twenty-three years' jail respectively. The main charges were kidnapping and attempted murder. I'm sure my testimony, delivered from my wheelchair, garnered support from the jury. They didn't stand a chance, and neither should they have.

It was a long haul for me, first recovery, then rehabilitation, and mostly, you know, these days it's not too bad. Truth be told, I have my dark days, and whether that's self-pity or a side effect of the pain killers I eat constantly, I can't say. Honestly, though, mostly, it's okay; I get by.

The bank gave me a reward of a ten-thousand-dollar bank account with them, which was a surprise. My best day was when I was awarded the prime minister's medal for bravery, and my family, along with friends and work clients, were there to see it. I was also a nominee for Australian of the Year, probably because of all the publicity the whole thing caused. Thank God I didn't win it because while I enjoyed the fame for a day when I got my medal, I never truly felt worthy of it. I just did what I did, and never thought I was brave. I believe most people would have done the same in my place.

You know, for me, the worst thing about the whole episode? Mina and I lost our best friends and neighbors. They moved away, not able to face living in their house anymore. But that wasn't the worst, because we understood their need to do that. It was, I think, every time they saw me, unable to walk, they felt so guilty. To my mind, they never should have felt that way, yet they did, and no amount of reassurance from me could change their minds.

These days I still work. A chartered accountant can work from a wheelchair, and almost all my clients waited for my recovery, which I found humbling. My car has had hand controls fitted, so I'm mobile and independent. Personal fitness is vital for a person with paraplegia, so I took up archery, and of all things, Mina and I bought a kayak, and we often go for a paddle down the river when the weather is kind.

All in all, life is good, and sure beats the alternative.

So you tell me, should I have picked up the note I saw lying in the puddle?

Three Ghosts

by

Julie Howard

Her daughter once told her: *If anyone in our family ever committed a murder, it would be you.*

Anna walked with her daughter along the sandy river path, trying to spot baby owls in the trees. Keen eyesight was necessary to become accomplished in this type of work. The brown-gray owlets huddled in their brown-black nests, hidden deep within the branches of brown-green trees. Anna made a competition out of who could find a nest first, who could find a nest with the most baby birds, or who could find the prettiest ones. That last category always led to a series of heated debates for the walk home.

When her Josie reached the age of eight years, it became great fun. Anna's heart expanded in her chest, at long last finding the cherished love she'd sought in the company of her children. As her daughter ran ahead, skirts flapping at her heels, Anna dreamed a wondrous future for her child: marriage to a kind man, a house with real glass windows, and a helper to tote water to the kitchen door.

Escape from these mountains.

By the time her daughter was fourteen, these debates along the river path were the only way they communicated. A gravitas had crept into their subjects; there were words in each of their throats that were never voiced. The exchanges gave them something to say to each other, allowing the maturing girl a way to disagree with her mother without creating a permanent rift.

Anna understood Josie would soon be married, with a home of her own and she'd need a tough skin to endure the years to come. It was a mother's job to prepare her children for the life ahead.

Which brought them to the topic of murder.

On the far side of the mountain, they'd heard, a gold miner had been killed over a dispute on his claim. The man slain was digging in a spot two feet over into another man's claim. One thing led to another. Or maybe this was just a story people told over the long, persistent winter to pass the time, allowing it to become more real and more bloody their minds as they waited for spring to unfold.

Anna and Josie discussed the possibility of killing a man over something so trivial as two feet of dirt when Josie brought the subject closer to home.

"Is gold worth so much?" she asked. "Are all men so violent? Does evil visit the hearts of us all?"

And then: "Who would be the likeliest killer in our family?" Josie stopped and stared at the river as she asked this last question, then answered it for herself. "If anyone in our family committed a murder, it would be you."

Anna turned away, trembling.

"I'm not sure," Anna told her after they'd walked on a bit farther. She knew straight away of who in their family was most prone to bloodshed, but let the speculation go on. "What about your father?"

Josie laughed. "Oh no," she said right away, though something at the edge of her tone rang as bitter and ironic. "Not a chance."

Still, the words pricked at Anna's image of herself as the more kindhearted and stable parent. It was without a doubt her husband was more likely than her to carry out this greatest of sins. They'd all witnessed his rages, face twisting and flushing red, the shouts, and stomping feet. Anna had tiptoed around her husband's moods for years. She would tuck her children in at night, lingering in their room long after their breaths became deep and even, while Frank fumed alone in the other room. Josie and her son Caleb were the best part of her. She saw promising futures for both her children stretching far into the coming century. *If only,* she thought. *If only*.

"Definitely your father." Anna's lips went thin as she spoke. "He'd murder me in a moment."

Josie looked at her mother, taking in her tight, still face, hearing the cold determination in her tone. The daughter gazed away, to the river swollen with new snow melt from the mountaintops. In another couple of weeks, the water would spill its banks and block the path until the mountain had fully shed its winter coat.

"Definitely you," Josie said, watching the rising river.

****

She and Frank met at a barn dance. Anna was thirteen and her mother was still eight months from the fever and cough that would take her away. As the dance was held in midsummer, heat filled the barn, generating streams of sweat off brows and backs. Anna watched her parents reel and whirl, feeling their love for each other radiate across the room.

She perched on a hay bale and plucked pieces of straw from her skirts, content to watch and admire the energy of the affair. Fiddle bows flying, hems sweeping, mouths laughing, and no possibility of hearing anything above the din. Anna had never been in a room with so

117

many people, with so much noise and so much to see.

Frank was eighteen, tall and lanky with a strong jaw that drew her attention over and over. Flattered by her open appreciation, he soon joined her on the hay bale.

"You don't dance?" he shouted over the boisterousness surrounding them.

Stunned that he was sitting next to her, she looked at her feet and shook her head, mute. She'd felt his gaze travel over her and a heat rose up inside her that she was sure would light the barn on fire. Frank shifted on the bale and then rose. He bent over her, and she smelled his heavy scent, dark and earthy.

"Well, you're a pretty little thing," he said near her ear, then left her to dance with others.

Anna watched him all night from her spot. She thought about him every day for the next year. When he rode up to the house to talk to her father, offering sympathies for their loss of her mother, she believed she'd conjured his appearance.

In those days, in the far mountains, girls were women at first blood; being given away was a literal transaction. The three of them said a prayer together, then she gathered her belongings. Anna's father helped her mount the extra horse Frank had brought with him for the occasion of gaining a wife. She glanced back only once at the home where she'd known so much happiness before turning shining eyes back to her husband.

****

Josie came along when Anna was just shy of sixteen, the birthing a violent experience. After the seventh hour of blood and screams, Frank walked out across the sunlit fields even as Anna pleaded with him not to leave her side. She thought of the lambs her father raised and how the mother sheep panted in their labor, their sides twitching and heaving. *I'm a sheep*, she thought over and over. *I'm a sheep.*

By the time Frank returned, stars had been in the skies for hours and Josie lay next to her. Words wouldn't form in her mouth so Anna bleated at Frank and he wrinkled his nose.

"Stinks like a pig carcass in here." He grabbed a blanket from the foot of the bed. "I'll sleep in the barn."

Caleb's birth came easier, three years later. She washed the sheets and started dinner before Frank returned later that day and, this time, she received a nod of approval. Later she wondered if he was acknowledging his son or that she hadn't inconvenienced him with her labors.

Her children's distinct personalities matched their appearance. Josie had Frank's dark hair and flash temper. Caleb was light in spirit and countenance. Anna was wild about both of them.

When Caleb was seven, Frank took him deer hunting. Anna had protested, saying he was too young, but Frank didn't bother with a response. He simply packed up the horses, camping gear and guns, before he and Caleb rode off for a three-day trip.

Anna looked out the window the next morning when she heard horses stamping their hooves, noses blowing against the cold. Frank sat atop his horse, saying not a word while Caleb dismounted and led his horse to the barn. Frank then turned his horse and disappeared again down the road. She ran to the barn where she found Caleb sobbing.

"I didn't want to shoot." He threw himself into her arms. "I didn't want to kill it."

She wrapped her arms around his thin, quaking body, smelling the sweetness of his hair. "Hush," she murmured. "There's always next year."

He pulled away and looked at her with horror. "I won't. I'll never kill it!"

Anna took a deep breath, but said nothing. Frank would never stand for a son who wasn't willing to kill.

No matter. There were more hunting trips, and by the time Caleb was eleven he'd become a crack shot. Her son, once sunshine, became midnight. His rare smiles worked slowly across his face as though each was an effort to produce.

Josie fared better, as if she'd been born to this type of life – surly father, angry brother, and damaged mother. She trudged from day to day, helping Anna and avoiding her father. It was only at night, in their shared room that Josie would laugh with her brother, teaching him his letters. The siblings would whisper their hopes and plans together as the moon rose to its peak and stars blanketed the sky.

****

Crimson, yellow, and orange leaves rained down furiously the week before the murder. Autumn arrived with a vengeance, not its usual softening transition from summer, but rather with a razor sharp edge. People remarked on the unusual weather, giving them a reason to talk to each other as they passed on the narrow farm roads. It made them worry what it meant for the impending winter, and they hurried to patch the roofs they'd delayed repairing for years.

Anna rubbed the bruise under one arm, then poked it with a finger, exploring. The ache had eased over the last week although the mark was still greenish, fading into yellow. Like the leaves on the ground, the colors on the bruise had been vivid and precipitated by a seasonal disturbance. The ones on her face were worse, screeching out the secrets of her marriage for all to see, to shame her before her children and neighbors.

A perfect ripe plum of a handprint, her nose pushed to one side, sixteen years of private marital discord revealed in a painful, humiliating way.

Frank talked louder and laughed harder that week, as though to cover his domestic crime with commotion. His boots thudded over the wooden planks of the house. Even the way his eyes darted from Josie to Caleb as he spoke echoed off the walls.

Anna watched her children withdraw into themselves and felt helpless to comfort them. Her presence was the source of their pain. At night, they shut her out of their room, saying they were too old to have their mother tuck them in. She stood silent in the hall outside their door, barely breathing as she heard them whispering to each other.

She'd counted the layers of emotional scars built up on her children as they grew, as carefully as she counted the years until they would leave home. It was like digging a hole, where the dirt mounts on one side as it's emptied out of the hole. They didn't look to her for protection or comfort anymore. That gave her strength.

"Go sit over there," her daughter said, five days before the murder, when Anna wanted to sit by the fire.

Anna's body ached, her nose painfully set back into place. Frank looked up at Josie from beneath dark, heavy eyebrows, his expression curious. Anna always sat across from him at the fireplace, sharing its warmth. The children would sit on the floor at their feet or pull up a stool farther back where they'd feel the chill at their backs and feet.

"Go on now." Anna's tone was a gentle scolding. "Don't be foolish."

Josie didn't move, and Frank looked back into the fire.

"Josie," she said, but as soon as she heard the pleading tone at the edge of her voice, she knew the battle was lost. She dragged up a stool and sat next to Caleb, whose gaze flickered toward her feet and then back at the fire.

She tucked her hands under her armpits for warmth while, inside, the cold kernel that was Anna's heart thawed a bit. Her daughter had discovered her power and was ready for the world. Josie, at fifteen, was now a woman.

"A woman to be reckoned with." Anna whispered the words softly to herself, wondering what that would be like.

****

Two days before the murder, while Anna and Josie walked down the river path for the last time, she suggested it was time to consider marriage. Anna put one foot in front of the other, feeling the ache in her hips and knowing time was growing short.

"Jacob's had his eye on you," she said.

"I'm not marrying anyone." Josie's tone was curt and final.

Anna pushed down the fear bubbling up inside her chest. "A woman alone," she started, then swallowed and started again. "A woman alone isn't safe in this world."

Josie made a sound in her throat.

"Whatever you think or want," Anna said, keeping

her voice devoid of emotion, "a woman needs a man. To have property, a house, children, anything at all."

Her daughter glanced at her with scorn, yet Anna felt Josie was listening. "I'd still have nothing." Josie spat out the words. "He'd have it."

They walked on, the ground sodden and quiet underfoot even as their shoes pressed the fallen leaves into the mud. Above, trees were going bare and empty nests dotted the branches.

"Widows can own property." Anna said this almost to herself, and Josie studied her mother's broken face.

They walked for another hour under the cavernous blue sky, neither saying another word. Anna's hips ached so much by the time they returned home that tears flowed rivers down her face.

Josie walked ahead of her into the house

****

The night of the murder, rain thundered on the roof and nearly drowned the first and only howl.

Anna ran outside, followed closely by Josie. Caleb, now sturdy and tall at twelve, stood over the body of his father, a shovel in his hand. Something dark and fleshy hung from the shovel, dripping a steady rhythm on the ground.

"Go inside," he ordered Anna. "I'll do this."

"Caleb," she whispered. The rain poured down, flattening her hair and drenching her clothing. Water filled her eyes and mouth.

Her heart broke for all that her children must have known. For the years she wore long sleeves in summer and muffled hcr cries in the night. Would Caleb blame her for this, for having to make a ruinous choice between mother and father? Would he hate her for her weakness in not taking up the shovel herself?

She stared down at the heap that had been her husband, then turned her back on him. Josie was back inside when she returned to the fire, her daughter's eyes accusing, mouth turned into a bitter frown.

Anna's plea came out high and broken. "What would you have had me do?"

Josie shook her head. "Not Caleb."

Anna turned to the window and saw her son's hunched back as he dragged the body toward the river. Her breath ran quick, and she looked back to Josie. Face grim, her daughter stared fixedly into the fire. Whatever her husband had done, she knew this was the future *she'd* created for the three of them.

He is dead, thought Anna, *but we are three ghosts.*

****

Her children left, never to return. 1870 passed in a blur; 1880 ushered in her first gray hairs. An abandoned woman is an object of pity and disdain, and neighbors stayed away. There were rumors, stories that grew and shape-shifted, but no body was found. Winter came, as did spring, summer and fall. Then, again.

Anna chopped wood, raised the chickens, hauled water, and oversaw a small crop of hay that a neighbor harvested in exchange for certain favors. Her body grew lean and muscular. Her hips no longer ached, although her nose still sat a bit crooked on her face.

Sometimes, she laughed out loud, long and hard. The stories in the long valley changed and people now talked about the old lady whose husband left her, turning her a little touched in the head. Anna had never been happier than as a ghost, that most lowly of all creatures.

One day, Josie came home. She was a large woman

now, dress tight at her bosom and hips, and she'd grown tall. She wore heavy boots and rode astride with authority. Anna felt pride when Josie swung down to the ground.

"A woman to be reckoned with," she said in greeting to her daughter.

Josie nodded, her eyes coursing over her mother's hair, its darkness faded into gray. "Touched in the head," she responded.

Anna shrugged and beckoned her daughter inside the house.

"Where's the furniture?" Josie asked.

The first years alone were hard ones. Felling a tree for wood was difficult business, and, besides, ghosts didn't need much warmth to survive.

"Burned it," Anna said. The memories of sitting by the fire with Caleb and Josie at her back, of her children whispering in the night, all so long ago, threatened to overwhelm her.

Josie sat on a tree stump that acted as a chair. Her third year alone, Anna hitched her horse to the tree, then dragged it across the fields to the house. It took her a week to cut off long branches and to chop the trunk into usable stumps, her hands bloody by the time she'd finished. That winter, by the fire, she sanded and carved at the stumps, then placed cushions on top. She was proud of her handiwork, but Josie made no comment.

"Did you get married?" Anna asked, sitting across from her grown girl, looking down at her hands. "Like we talked about?"

Josie shook her head. "No need. Laws are changing. I have my own place in Fairfield. And a good woman, too."

Anna puzzled at that for a moment, not comprehending, and then she gave her daughter a startled look. "How do you live?" she asked. "For money?"

Josie raised her chin. "Sarah teaches," she said. "I raise pigs. It's a good life."

Anna heard the happiness in her daughter's voice, and she wiped away a tear that caught her unawares. There was more to say, she knew, but she didn't know how to talk to people anymore. Josie waited, hands folded in her lap, her eyes alert and glancing around the room.

"Caleb?" The question came out from somewhere deep inside Anna's heart. Her body trembled while she waited for the answer.

"He went out to California," Josie said with a nod toward the western mountain. "Last letter he sent mentioned a few kids – guess there must be a wife, too."

It was too much to take in all at once. A letter sent. Children. A wife.

"What does he do there, in California?" Her mind kept circling around letters sent between her children, that they'd kept in touch with each other. No letters to her, of course, but it was enough.

Josie gave a harsh laugh. "He took up with a gang for awhile. Robbed some banks. Bought a farm with the money and turned respectable."

Anna remembered Caleb's crying in the barn over shooting a deer, his soft hair, the way he smelled when she tucked him in at night. She nodded. "A farm," she said. "That's good. Land is good."

"You taught us right." Josie's tone was crisp, brittle. "About survival."

An image of a dripping shovel in the rain came into Anna's head. Afterward, Josie's rage and Caleb's refusal to talk. By the end of that week, her children were gone.

"Three ghosts," she said to the fire.

"Mama." Josie's voice broke on the word. "You come on with me now."

Anna drew a breath and then forced another through her lungs. She dipped her head, more gray than not these days. Most of her life gone.

"Too late for me." Anna shook her head. "I'm glad for you, though. And Caleb."

Josie just nodded.

****

They had dinner and she told her mother about the pig business, how little piglets fought and wiggled for life from the start and how they grew to enormous proportions. Anna's eyes glowed and her chest ached as she watched her daughter talk.

"In my county, there's talk of a woman who's lived ninety-five years and still going strong," Josie said, glancing up at her mother and then back down at her plate. "How old are you, mama?"

Anna breathed for a few moments, trying to remember. "Forty-nine. Last week."

"Imagine that," Josie said in a wondering tone. "Half your life ahead yet."

****

Josie slept in her old room, her childhood blankets tucked to her chin. Anna stood in the doorway, moonlight illuminating the rise and fall of her daughter's chest, rumbling snores falling like music on her ears. She thought about Caleb writing letters and pigs and her daughter's lover.

She mostly thought about how her children had fought their way back from a ghostly world into substantial lives.

In the morning, Josie tucked her belongings back in her satchel and turned to her mother with sad eyes to say goodbye.

"That woman, who's ninety-five," started Anna.

Josie waited, silent. The door creaked open from a breeze and swung lightly on its hinges. From across the fields, the sound of the river could be heard, a steady rushing that headed forever downstream.

"Is she me?" Anna asked.

Josie's lips trembled and she swallowed. "Could be."

Anna gave a quick nod. Josie waited by the door as Anna tucked her meager possessions into an old flour sack. Mother and daughter worked efficiently to saddle Anna's horse and chase the chickens into the fields to find their own destinies.

They rode along the river path, and Anna turned her head only once to look back to the place she'd haunted for so many years.

She wondered what wild tale people would tell about her later. How her family had disappeared one by one, vanishing, vanishing ghosts all.

Detective Paws
and Lip Gloss

by

Maureen L. Bonatch

Catherine snapped her phone shut, ignoring the messages. When would her father accept that she would be fine living on her own? She signaled the bartender for her tab.

A heavy hand landed on her shoulder. She sighed, expecting it to be her brother checking up on her. Since Mom died, the males in her family had become suffocating in their overprotectiveness. It was as if they thought she needed to be in a bubble in order to keep her safe from any harm. Moving out had been only the first step to prove she could handle her life independently.

When she swiveled her bar stool, the comment already locked and loaded, aimed at her brother, died on her lips when she came face to face with a stranger.

"Shirley, why'd you do it?" The woman asked, her voice slurring.

"Pardon me?" The strong smell of alcohol and sweat made Catherine cringe back a bit. "I'm not—"

"It's too late, now." The woman crumpled like a discarded tissue, folding her arms to rest her head on the bar.

"Um, what's too late?"

The woman's hand shot forward to grasp at a shot glass filled with an amber liquid and toppled it onto Catherine's lap.

"Oh!" Catherine jerked when the liquid soaked her skirt.

The woman lifted her head and shook a dirt-encrusted finger at Catherine. "Your fault, ya know. I looked but couldn't find him."

Catherine frowned, already regretting the quick stop at the bar before going home. "I don't know what you're—"

"Shirley, why?" Tears leaked from the stranger's red-rimmed eyes. "You didn't have to kill him. Tell me where he's buried, please."

"What?" Surely the booze was causing this woman to embellish. "I'm not Shirley." Catherine took a closer look at the hands of the stranger as heads began to turn in interest toward the scene. The woman's nails were ragged and torn, knuckles cracked and bleeding.

"Where in the park? I need to know." The woman pounded her fist on the bar, and Catherine's wine glass teetered until she seized the stem. "I want to plant some daisies there."

The woman swiped at her face with the back of one hand, leaving a streak of dirt. "They were his favorite." As she dropped her arm, this time she knocked a basket of peanuts to the floor.

That brought the bartender over in a flash. "Little lady," he warned Catherine, "you need to get your friend outta here before I call the cops." He glared at them and slapped a bill down on the bar. "She's disturbing my customers."

"She's not my friend. I don't even know her." This wasn't the way she hoped to meet some people near her new apartment. If this drunk woman represented the populace of her new neighborhood, it would only prove that her father was right. That she'd chosen a bad part of town to live alone. Sure, it would've been okay for her brothers, but not for her.

Catherine tried to rise from the stool, but the woman slid into the seat beside her and clutched her arm with both hands until she pulled free. "Let me go."

The bartender eyed them, shaking his head, and nodding toward the door.

Like she needed the cops showing up here. This was her brother's beat. It was the only way her father had agreed she could move out. Or worse, Rob Stevens could answer the call. This wasn't the first impression she wanted to make on the gorgeous cop who'd caught her eye a few months ago.

"Sure, you called me your little Jo-Jo. That's why you killed him. You were just jealous." The woman's beady eyes glistened with hate. "He loved me! Now you can't even remember my name." Spittle spewed from her mouth and ran down her chin,

Catherine pulled back at the gust of stinking breath accompanying the saliva. "You've mistaken me for someone else." She hopped down from the stool and walked away as the woman's cries filled her ears.

"It's Joann. I thought I was your little Jo-Jo. Shirley, don't leave me!"

She peeked over her shoulder to see the woman sliding off the bar stool as if to begin pursuit. Instead, she slid down to the floor and began to wail.

Ducking into the sanctuary of the women's restroom, Catherine breathed a sigh of relief. Maybe she could wait it out until the bouncers took care of the drunk. She sighed, or better yet, she should try to see if she could help her out. If she really was a cop, like her brother, that's what she'd do. She walked over to the mirror.

"Oh, that's just great." Catherine set her brand-new

133

designer purse on the counter. She brushed at the dirt on her blouse, where the woman had pawed her, but her efforts only widened the smear. She fruitlessly dabbed at her sodden skirt. "I wouldn't have had to waste my money on clothes for the office if I could've followed my original plan and went into the police academy."

Granted, she wouldn't have had to spend so much money on her clothes. She could've bought something less expensive but she'd been angry at her father for refusing to recommend her for the academy. Some retail therapy seemed like a good solution at the time, but she'd paid for her little act of rebellion with almost an entire paycheck.

The click of a stall door echoed off the white barren walls. She jumped. For some reason she thought she was alone. Catherine raised her eyes to the mirror and frowned into the dim lighting. At first it appeared that a hulk of a man was strolling out of the stall. An instant later she realized it was a woman, with her eyes narrowed as she fixed Catherine with a dark gaze.

"Uh, hi." Catherine snatched one more paper towel from the pile and moved rapidly toward the door. One cranky drunk she could handle, but two had her calling it a night. Besides, this one didn't look drunk, she looked angry.

"She told you," the he-woman murmured. "She must like you...ya know." The woman bared her rotting teeth in a feeble attempt at a smile.

Catherine froze when she arrived at the trash can, noting the speckles of...something splattered over the woman's overalls embroidered with the name, Shirley.

"She liked him, too...ya know." Shirley lumbered a few steps closer, her gaze fixed on Catherine.

Catherine backed toward the exit, not taking her gaze off of Shirley.

"She's mine…ya know." The giant began to walk towards her. "My little Jo-Jo."

"The drunk at the bar?" Catherine winced at her poor choice of words. "Really, I'm not interested. You can have her."

"What, you too good for her, city girl?" The he-woman cocked her head while her gaze roamed over Catherine, lingering on her legs and then her breasts.

Catherine clutched her hands around herself, feeling tiny and exposed.

"Um, no, it's not that—" When her buttocks met the door, Catherine shoved it open, spun around, and then rushed out into the bar.

****

Despite her three-inch heels, Catherine ran home faster than she'd realized she was capable of doing. It felt like she couldn't breathe, or feel safe, until she'd finally slammed the door of her apartment shut. She leaned against it, closing her eyes. Her heart hammered as she sucked in much needed oxygen.

She grabbed the receiver from the landline phone and dialed the first three numbers before stopping suddenly, holding it in her hand.

"Fraidy cat," Catherine murmured. She could hear the jeers of her brothers once they got wind of this. That's what she got, for being the only girl in a family of cops. She replaced the phone against the cradle.

"I'm probably overreacting." Which is exactly what her father and brothers would say. There was no way they'd believe her story about not one, but two crazy women at the bar singling her out. Besides, she never liked playing the damsel in distress role. She wanted to be the one who rescued the damsel and the dude.

She examined the broken heel she'd acquired after running the second block of the four blocks home. "Shoot." They were brand-new and she couldn't afford another pair. She'd invested almost all of her savings into her new place.

"Hey Sherlock." Catherine crouched down to pet her basset hound who ambled over to greet her. He was as close as she would get to a partner, being that her police captain father didn't think his baby girl could hack being a cop. So, for now, she was stuck being a paralegal until she could prove him wrong.

"No, I'm not calling," Catherine informed Sherlock as he studied her with sad, soulful eyes. She glanced at the boxes still lining the wall. "I'll be fine on my own, really." As if agreeing with her, the hound thumped his tail with gusto.

"That's right. *We'll* be fine." Catherine reassured Sherlock, as if he was the one who needed to hear that.

Catherine glanced around, her brow furrowed. "Hey, have you seen my purse?"

The ringing of the phone interrupted her search. Catherine frowned when she saw her cell phone number on the caller ID. "What? How is someone calling my apartment with my cell phone?"

Realization dawned, causing a chill to run through her body as she picked up the receiver. Before she could speak, a voice said, "Hi Catherine Jones, at 222 Hemlock Avenue, Apartment 23, you forgot something... ya know," the voice taunted.

She slammed the receiver down and rushed to the window. "Shit." She didn't see anyone lurking outside, but that didn't mean much. The glow of the streetlights was limited, and left many dark shadows that could conceal Jo-Jo the drunk and Shirley, the he-woman.

The phone rang again. She whirled around to face it, tensing as she let the answering machine pick it up.

"Listen, city girl, you've got some information I want back...ya know." The phone line hissed and crackled.

Catherine disconnected the call, but the phone rang again. She looked at Sherlock in desperation. The machine picked up again, and she began to pace, contemplating her situation.

"Don't like ya hangin' up on me like that, ya know. Problem is that the information I need is in your head, city girl. Jo-Jo likes to talk too much. Just how do I go about gettin' that information out of there?"

Catherine unplugged the phone from the wall. When she slumped to the floor Sherlock nudged her side, and she stroked him—drawing comfort from his presence. "I know John's on duty tonight, but if I call him he's sure to call Dad. They'll think I can't handle myself." Catherine sighed, wondering if they weren't right.

Sherlock looked distressed, but then again, as a basset hound, he usually did.

She ran her hand through her hair. "I'll never get to go to the academy and worse, I'll be back living at home."

"I have an idea. Maybe this is my chance." She jumped up, startling Sherlock, and then rushed to her bedroom. Minutes later she emerged in sweats and sneakers. Sherlock instantly became as animated as his sloth-like self was able to and tottered over to pick up his leash in his jowls.

"Sorry buddy, not tonight." She patted his head. "Time to do some detective work and I have to do this on my own."

Her wannabe partner in crime-fighting whined pitifully.

Catherine hesitated, then decided to take him, if only for moral support. "Okay buddy, but if the going gets tough I'm counting on outrunning them, so you'll need to find a good hiding spot."

She clipped on a fanny pack, scowling with irritation that her father wouldn't let her keep a gun. "You'd be more likely to shoot yourself, Cat," Catherine muttered in an imitation of her father's disapproving tone.

Catherine tossed in a can of mace, a flashlight, and her spare cell phone. Her father had insisted she keep her old cell phone because it could still be used to call 911 and for once she was grateful she'd listened. A pair of handcuffs completed her stash. She flushed as she recalled their use with her last boyfriend.

After surveying the items, she shrugged and threw in a tube of lip gloss. She never left home without it, so why start now?

She jotted a note to her family, detailing the evenings events and the possibility that someone had been murdered. Just in case, she told herself. As she knelt by Sherlock, she contemplated the only reason the note would be necessary. "Nope. Not going to happen." She shook her head, pushing away thoughts of being maimed and death.

The note went into the ID section of Sherlock's collar. As if sensing her anxiety, he began to lick her face. She patted his head in gratitude and clipped on his leash. "It's just in case things go wrong, buddy. Don't worry. We aren't going to need it." She nodded, trying to convince herself trying to find a grave, and the possibility of running into two deranged women in the dark was a good idea.

"We'll go down to the park and see if there is anything suspicious-looking that could be a fresh grave. If we do, then we'll call John and ask him to take a look. I need to validate there is something more involved than the rantings of two drunk women so I don't look like an idiot." She realized she'd need to call John either way— they had her purse which had her identification, and her address. She shuddered. Her apartment suddenly didn't feel as safe.

Sherlock whined.

"Okay, you're right," Catherine said with a sigh. "It's a weak plan. If we happen to meet up with Shirley, I'll spray her with the mace. While she's distracted, I'll cuff her and then call John. Either way, Dad won't think I'm overreacting when I have evidence of foul play."

It sounded like a good plan. At least in theory.

Catherine paused at her apartment door to squint through the peek hole. She expelled the air she didn't realize she'd been holding when she didn't encounter Shirley's beady eyes and nasty face glaring back at her from the hall. She threw open the door with a flourish before she lost her courage. She scanned the empty hallway.

"Okay Sherlock, It's go time." The two of them slunk out into the night.

****

Catherine's false bravado began to fade when she and Sherlock entered the park area where the street lights were less prevalent. Crickets screamed like a chorus gone mad, and the trees that seemed so warm and welcoming in the daylight now cast sinister shadows. She pulled Sherlock a little closer. At least he seemed oblivious to the dangers of the night and appeared to just be happy to be out on a walk.

Catherine jumped when an owl hooted. "Maybe this wasn't such a good idea, Sherlock. Let's take one quick look and then we're out of here." Peering around with her flashlight, her eyes widened when she spotted some yellow daisies planted in a large mound of fresh dirt.

"Who-hoo, Sherlock! Detective work is easier than I thought." Catherine rushed over to the daisies with Sherlock trotting beside her.

"You're right, ya know. This was easy," Shirley said, lumbering out from the shadows.

Catherine's flashlight first caught on her stolen purse, which looked so out of place on the he-woman, then the huge hand clutching it—an appendage that could easily snap her neck and every other bone in her body. She backed up, avoiding the fresh dirt which may already be a crime scene, or possibly become one if Shirley had her way.

She dropped Sherlock's leash while fumbling for the can of mace. All the time cursing herself for making a rookie mistake by rushing in without surveying the scene. As Shirley crossed the mound of dirt without hesitation, the mace popped right out of Catherine's sweaty grip and rolled off into the night. In desperation, she grabbed the lip gloss.

Catherine dodged to the side when Shirley lunged and stepped behind the beastly woman. She jammed the lip gloss into Shirley's back with force, as if it were a gun. "Don't move, sasquatch, or you're dead."

Shirley's laugh was deep and harsh. "Go ahead, city girl. Don't think ya got it in ya."

"Try me." Catherine kept up the charade by pushing the lip gloss into Shirley's back so hard that the end snapped off.

Shirley stumbled forward, her yell sounded as if Catherine had only managed to make her furious.

Catherine staggered back, confused at how the lip gloss could've pushed Shirley further into a rage until she heard ferocious growling. When she looked down, she noted Sherlock firmly latched onto Shirley's ankle.

Jumping in to help, she gave her a shove, and the he-woman toppled over while Sherlock kept his jaws clamped tight. While her fearless partner held the perp, Catherine pulled out the handcuffs and secured them onto Shirley's ankles—fearful that if she got too close to those meaty hands that Shirley would gain the advantage.

She pulled out her cell phone to call her brother, but someone or something crashed against her hip. Catherine and the phone went tumbling to the ground. The smell of booze and sweat confirmed the drunk from the bar, Joann, was the culprit.

But Catherine wasn't her intended target.

While Shirley cursed and Joann screamed, Catherine crawled on her belly to retrieve her flashlight and then rolled over and directed the light to the scene in front of her.

Joann was wrestling with Shirley on the mound of fresh dirt.

"You ruined my daisies!" she screeched, pulling at Shirley's hair while Shirley tried to push her off.

"Jo-Jo, get off. I don't wanna hurt ya," He-woman

bellowed.

As the dirt scattered, Catherine's flashlight caught on something…

Peering closer, she saw a human nose sprouting from the earth. Joann's hysterical screams filled the night as she looked at her lover's face gazing up at her from the grave.

The sight caused Catherine's stomach to roil and she scrambled around trying to locate the missing phone. Suddenly, a bright light washed over her face, and she shielded her eyes with her hand.

"Break it up. This is the police."

Catherine held her hands in the air and yelled, "Over here! Those women over there, officer. They have a body buried there."

"Ms, are you injured?" the policeman asked, approaching her.

"No, I'm…" Catherine looked down and saw the streaks of red all over her hands and shirt. "Um, it's just lip gloss."

"Stay on the ground. I've called for backup," the policeman commanded as he went over to contend with Shirley and Joann.

It just figured that Rob Stevens, the hottest policeman at the station, would be the one to find her in this condition. Sherlock came over to sit beside her. Catherine whispered praises and promises of indulgent treats for his heroic behavior.

The arrival of additional officers was announced by car doors slamming, and the night sky illuminated with a plethora of flashing lights.

"Cat?" She heard someone say, then recognized her brother, John's, voice. He bent down to help her up.

"What in the world are you and Sherlock doing out here in the park? In the middle of the night? You could've been killed."

Catherine steeled herself for the customary lecture, but while waiting for his ranting to cease she was mercifully saved by the hunky Rob Stevens.

"John you should be commending her," Rob said, his expression serious. He stood with his thumbs looped through his belt loops.

She stared at Rob with her mouth gaping open in shock. "Commending?"

"She had this scene pretty much under control when I arrived," Rob looked to Catherine and winked.

"But, how?" John stuttered as their father rushed up to them.

Catherine stood up straighter and held up her weapon. "Why, with a tube of lip gloss. Dad, I guess you were right." She shrugged. "I didn't need a gun."

All three men studied the broken lip-gloss tube in silence and obvious confusion, perhaps pondering the mysteries of women and the true purpose of cosmetics.

Another officer approached. "Ms. Jones, where did you get these handcuffs?"

Catherine flushed, grateful that she didn't have to answer that embarrassing question when Rob intervened.

"She's going to be a wonderful addition to the force, sir," he said, giving Catherine a warm smile. "I'll be glad to help mentor her. Err, that is, if it's okay with you, sir."

"What? Why, I…" Catherine's father sputtered.

"Don't worry, Dad, there's plenty of time to think about it before the academy opens for fall enrollment," her brother spoke up.

"That's right, you do have some time, Dad, and

thanks Rob for the offer, but I already have a partner. Catherine reached down, picked up Sherlock, and without giving the three men another thought, she planted a big kiss on Sherlock's nose.

The Ring

by

Margaret Ann Spence

The day after the storm, the sun glared as if angry it had been denied even an hour of blasting the summer-weary neighborhood with its heat. Making the point, steam rose from the pavements. Everything was super-light, as when the ophthalmologist dilates your eyes. That's when Suzanne saw, looking out the french doors to the battered lawn, the glitter.

She put down her coffee cup and stepped outside into the streaming light. She picked her way through the debris, kicked the fallen twigs and leaves on the sodden grass. The glint drew her. A sparkle in the grass.

A diamond engagement ring lay capsized on the ground.

Lucky one of the birds hasn't got it, she marveled as she picked it up. Who did it belong to? She herself had never had an engagement ring; it was a luxury she and her husband had foregone at the time, and she had never regretted it.

She slipped it in her pocket.

They'd been good savers, Chad and she, and the money they could have spent on a ring went into their savings for the house down payment.

Now they owned a house. A modest house to be sure, in a subdivision on a tree-lined street. She'd made it pretty, too. She learned to upholster chairs and sofas she found at garage sales. She was a terrific paint stripper, and old dressers were burnished now, the beauty of their natural wood revealed, or sometimes, if the wood was not so beautiful, a coat or two or three of bright-colored paint made them like new.

Not that Chad noticed her improvements. He didn't seem to have the beauty gene. She put it down to his impoverished childhood. As far as Chad was concerned, home ownership was a sign of status. He wanted to save and move up the property ladder.

"One day, Suze," he told her, "one day we'll have a big house with a pool. A three-car garage."

For now, of course, they only needed the one car. Chad didn't really like her to go out without him. She understood. It was a matter of pride for him to be able to support a wife, something his own father had never been able to do. So, she shopped locally, grew much of their own produce in her prolific veggie patch. She'd have to inspect that later. No doubt the beans and the lettuce had taken a battering. But nature was resilient, and in a few days the vegetables would recover. What was a little knocking about, after all?

Suzanne righted an upside-down patio chair and positioned a trash bag on its metal frame.

"First thing," she said out loud, "is to clean up the rest of the yard." A familiar pressure pushed her to pick up a rake as she surveyed the wreckage. Pieces of wood, strips of canvas from someone's ramada, a few twisted scraps of metal, a broken outdoor lamp littered the yard. It would take a good two hours of piling the wheelbarrow with broken branches, sticks, and leaves even after she got rid of the junk. She'd have to get rid of the mess before Chad saw it. She began piling the broken objects in a corner of the yard. She would find a way to use these found objects, she was sure.

Her hand fingered the ring in her pocket.

A shiver ran through her. That ring had belonged to someone. She doubted that it had actually flown off someone's hand, but had it been in a drawer, or on a windowsill, removed from a housewife's hands as she did the dishes? It was about dinner time when the storm had struck last night.

What should she do? Hand it to the police? No. They had enough to do and were not a lost and found office. Put a notice on Craigslist? Too dangerous. Pawn it? Too tacky. Place a classified ad? Hardly. If someone answered an ad for a "lost ring," how on earth could she verify the ring was theirs?

No. She would keep the ring. She would not tell Chad. He wouldn't approve, either of the ring itself or her self-indulgence. Even what he might call her dishonesty. But who was she really hurting if she kept the ring? The ring's rightful owner could claim the loss on her own insurance. Wasn't that the point of insurance?

If she sold the ring, she could use it to add to the fix-up-the-house fund. Yes, that was what she would do. She didn't work, and this would be her contribution to their future. It wouldn't be long now, Chad had promised, before they'd Move Up.

She ran a finger over the ring again. She smiled. What would it look like on her?

After washing it in the kitchen sink, she wiped the ring very carefully on a tissue. It shone and sparkled. She laid the ring gently on the counter and surveyed her own hands. Not pretty. The nails were ragged; if she wore nail polish, she'd chip it. She reached for a jar of hand cream. She rubbed it on her hands, sloping the greasy mix down into the webs of her fingers, rubbing it into the palm. Her hands, those chapped and grubby hands which did all that work she believed in. All that work of sustainability, of recycling, of hammering and sawing and digging in the garden. Of pummeling dough to make bread. A homesteading kind of life, even in a subdivision. She'd chosen it, pleased to be able to stretch every dollar Chad gave her for the housekeeping.

But here now, was a ring. A ring that belonged to someone else. Someone who thought a woman deserved a bit of luxury. More than a bit. This ring would be worth thousands.

How much? She'd have to get it appraised, or go to a jeweler to get an opinion. What if she wore it and someone at the supermarket barreled into her with the cart, splaying her hands before her, showing a pale band of skin where a ring once nestled, saying, I had a ring like that! I lost it in the storm! What could she say? That her fiancé had given it to her? That it was her mother's?

All of a sudden that didn't matter. She'd find a way. She wanted to wear the ring, now. The ring looked good on her finger. Would look even better with a bit of polish on her nails. She searched the medicine cabinet for nail polish. None.

She had to have lacquered nails in order to set off the ring. Not a problem. She needed to go shopping anyway.

Three hours later, Suzanne emerged from the shopping mall. Nail polish in reds and pale pinks nestled in a plastic bag. New underwear, or rather, lingerie, a more romantic name for what she'd purchased, lay flat in pale mauve tissue paper. A slimming black dress in a shiny boutique bag dangled from her left arm together with the lingerie, while in her right hand a bottle of champagne, pâté, and water crackers bulged from a shopping bag (canvas, reusable) together with the finest fillet steak.

Just this once, she'd make a little party for Chad and herself.

By five thirty she was ready. The house shone, every dust mote in every corner had been banished by the vacuum's wand. Even the windows were polished, the french doors gleaming as they opened to the patio. After her morning's work, the yard looked as good as new. Once she'd removed the broken stems, even the flowers had perked up, revived by the sun after the storm. A stillness hung in the air, a heavy, humid warmth.

She set the table. A cloth, two candles, two place settings with the pretty flower-sprigged plates she'd inherited from her mother. She went to a sideboard and removed a felt roll and a silver ice bucket. Unrolling the felted scroll, she admired the silverware she'd bought years ago at a yard sale. How she'd loved removing its tarnish so the forks and knives shone like a fish's fins. She gently lowered two wine glasses to the right of the plates, set the napkins on the left, and arranged the supermarket flowers artistically, tallest ones in the middle, the smaller ones on the side, in a glass vase.

Ice tinkled into the bucket, and she nestled the champagne bottle inside.

With a smile at her handiwork, she went into the master bedroom, where the beautiful new dress lay waiting on the bedspread. She took a shower. She hunted in the drawer of the vanity for the perfume she'd bought herself last Christmas (not telling Chad!) and slathered it on. The new lingerie under her slinky dress uplifted her breasts and slimmed her tummy. Her nails were buffed and polished, courtesy of those lovely Vietnamese girls at the Head to Toes salon, and she pulled her brushed and shiny hair into a smart chignon. A thin glaze of make-up sheened her face, and her lips glowed a glossy pink. She slipped her now-smoothed feet into shiny silver sandals.

Chad will be home soon, she thought as she poured herself the first glass of champagne. She spread a little pâté on a cracker and took a small bite. Another, and another glass of champagne. Her brain seemed fuzzy all of a sudden, and a glob of pâté slithered from the cracker down the silky front of her dress. Shame!

But Chad never noticed things like that, anyway. When he came home, he'd probably want to take that dress right off and ravish her right there on the living room floor. His hair was so blond, Chad's was, his body so muscled and trim. How hard she'd fallen for him when he'd eyed her, of all the girls in the school, that day by the lockers, so long ago. He was voted most likely to succeed and, when they were dating, had talked often of his ambition to rise above the trailer park he'd been born into.

And he had, of course. They both had, though her parents had hated the idea of her marrying this blond boy from nowhere and nothing. She had to hand it to him. He was so sure of his path, so determined not to follow the gambling and spendthrift habits of his parents. He would bring her with him, he told Suzanne, and make them rich. She'd never have to suffer like his mother had.

Where was he? She'd drunk the champagne now and opened a bottle of pinot noir. Maybe they wouldn't have the steak tonight. Yes, Chad seemed to be working late, and it would be a shame to waste an expensive piece of meat on an exhausted man. She wasn't hungry anyway. She took a sip of red wine and held her hand up to the light. The red lampshade gave her whole hand a pinky glow as she admired her ring and her shiny fingernails.

Those hands! Never had they looked so pretty, if she could just ignore the dark smudges on them. Age spots they called them. Never mind. She had her figure still.

She did a little twirl right there in the living room, her glass in hand. Chad's favorite music sounded softly from the stereo. Suzanne danced before it and tripped on the rug. The glass smashed. Red wine pooled on the floor, and Suzanne could see from her prone position wine had also flooded her silk dress, darkening it in a plummy stain.

She began to laugh. She couldn't cry, even though Chad would be angry if he saw her now, disheveled, out of control, drunk, and in a lascivious mood.

She sat up. She couldn't cry because she didn't have to.

Chad, with his fierce temper, his rigid beliefs, would not be coming home. She put her hand on the edge of the coffee table. Its sharp corner bit into her hand as she raised herself up. She stood, lowered her hands to the hem of her dress and raised it over her head. She took off her bra and panties, her frilly, laced, and very expensive underwear. Her eyes moved downwards. Her breasts sagged, her stomach was scored with pouches, and her thighs mapped with blue veins.

She looked down at her mottled feet. Her bunions had forced their way out of the side of the sandals. She kicked them off.

She left the dress, the soiled carpet, and the smashed glass and staggered to the bedroom. She lay on the bed, feeling very, very drunk and also sharply aware. How could the two things co-exist? Drunkenness and clarity. It was as if a membrane had been removed from her mind.

Chad was dead.

He'd been dead for months. A heart attack felled him in the shower. The EMTs asked why she hadn't called sooner. She didn't know he was in trouble, she told them. She'd been outside weeding the garden and didn't realize he wasn't in his favorite chair reading the Sunday paper till she'd come inside to make his coffee. Called and got no answer.

She didn't tell them she'd cleaned the kitchen, taking her peaceful time, before she went into the bathroom and found him.

The horror of it. The relief. The denial.

Chills went through her like an icy bath. He was dead. Really.

She didn't have to do what he wanted anymore. She looked at her hands, her manicured nails, and the third finger, left hand. Behind her wedding band something sparkled and gave her joy. She had the ring.

She'd keep it.

Portrait of a Gunfighter

by

Hywela Lyn

26th October 1881

Almost two hours after high noon. Freemont Street lies deserted, wilting in the fiery rays of the afternoon sun.

I draw back the lace curtains and peer through the window. The only sign of life is a single horse, a large bay, hitched to the rail on the other side of the street.

"We're gonna have to go now, honey."

The words, although spoken in a soft tone, startle me. I turn back from the window, to face the four men standing, waiting.

"Please—please don't go. Let the sheriff handle it."

"It's too late for that now, hun. You know it is. Sheriff Behan's worse'n useless. If he was goin' to stop it, he should've stepped in a long time ago."

I know, deep down, that he has to go, but it breaks my heart to think he might be going to his death. I look up at him, trying to smile, and cling to him briefly. "Go then, God be with you."

"We'll be all right, darlin'."

Another hand touches my arm. "Don't you worry none, sweet lady. We know what we're doing."

"Do you, Doc? Do you, really?" I bite my lip. I should know better than to talk sharp to men who are about to face such odds. "Be careful, please—all of you."

They move to the door, and I listen to their footsteps on the stairs, and the sound of the door closing as they step into the street. I turn back to the window.

With a dry mouth, I watch them stride resolutely to the appointed place. The marshal of this prosperous and infamous mining town and his three deputies—two brothers and the friend they call 'Doc'.

Doc's gaunt form is conspicuous in the butterfly colors of his gambler's garb against the somber blackness of the attire the others wear. He is, I believe, not yet thirty. It seems wrong for a man to die so young. This is how he wants it, though—in the company of friends, with a gun in his hand.

The thought places a knot of fear in my heart, and the breath catches in my throat. The fear I feel is not for him, though, fond of him as I am. It is for one of the other deputy marshals—my husband.

A small ball of tumbleweed bowls along the street, propelled by the light breeze. The horse tethered to the rail by the boardwalk shies skittishly, eyes rolling white-ringed, ears laid flat.

I look back to where the four men were, but a minute ago. They have turned the corner and I can no longer see them. In the silence, I cast my mind back to the first time he ever wore a marshal's star, or pulled a gun in the name of the law…

****

We stepped off the stage at Ellsworth, Kansas—one of the roughest, most lawless towns in the West—on a hot afternoon in August of '73. The town was terrorized by two men in particular, Texan gamblers, Bill and Ben Thompson, who had no respect for the local law enforcers.

This particular afternoon, a ruckus started up in the saloon. We dove for cover like everyone else. The

Thompson brothers were apparently after a third man, for a gambling debt. The sheriff, whose name was Whitney, said the man had left town. Bill Thompson fired off both barrels of his gun and killed Whitney in cold blood before mounting his horse and galloping away, covered by his brother, Ben.

Ben backed toward the saloon, brandishing his shotgun. His Texan cronies were all armed with six-shooters, and I guess he felt pretty safe.

"Nobody ain't goin' ter go after my brother," he yelled, "an' I'll kill the first man ter go fer the marshal."

However, the marshal and deputy marshal, it seemed, had no intention of making themselves sitting targets.

The mayor came out and called across the street to Thompson, telling him he was under arrest.

Thompson's response was a laugh, harsh and scornful.

My man and I had watched the incident from the safety of a doorway. Before I could stop him, my husband stepped up to the mayor and remarked that he did not think much of the local law enforcement. I made a move to join him, but he raised a hand, signalling me to stay where I was.

"An' who the hell're you anyway?" the mayor snapped.

"Only a casual observer, but I reckon if I was in your place, I'd arrest that man before he takes over this town."

This coming from a young man, dressed in city clothes, and wearing no gun, seemed to snap something inside the mayor. Wordlessly he took a marshal's badge from his pocket.

I gasped as I realised that I was about to become the

wife of the new marshal of Ellesworth.

"All right then, seeing as you're so eager—you do it, but you'd best get down to the store first and get yourself a pair of guns."

Within moments this stranger—my husband—had taken the oath and pinned on the marshal's badge.

I stood, speechless, stunned, watching as he entered the store to come out a few minutes later with a pair of worn-looking holsters and six-shooters. I found out afterward that the guns actually had hair triggers.

He loaded both guns with an air of calmness, then walked out onto the street toward the most dangerous and hardened gunman in those parts.

I sent up a silent prayer. The odds were so stacked against him. He hardly seemed aware of the cowboys behind Thompson, or the crowd gathered in the street to see the Texan kill this greenhorn stranger.

Thompson watched, standing with his feet apart and his shotgun held across his body, fingers curled around the trigger. He had only to swing the barrel around a little. He couldn't miss at that range. What chance did anyone, however fast he was, have against a man holding a loaded shotgun? He even seemed puzzled himself.

He called out, "What yer want, stranger? We ain't got no quarrel. Drop yer guns an' git back where yer belong."

"I've come to arrest you. Put your hands up and throw down your gun." The distance between the two men was now less than fifteen yards. Still, he closed in on the defiant criminal.

"Yer crazy—how exactly do yer aim to arrest me, huh?"

"If you don't come peaceably, I guess I'll have to

kill you."

"An' what if I kill you, huh?"

"You won't—because you'll be dead first. Oh, your friends might git me, after I've shot you, but *you* won't have time to turn that shotgun on me. At this distance, my friend, I'll git you easy enough."

Thompson's black eyes narrowed to mere slits. He did not look nearly as confident as a moment ago.

To my amazement, and I suppose, that of everyone else, Thompson threw his gun into the road and raised his hands. Even his cowboy friends seemed too surprised to go for their guns.

I didn't see him draw, but somehow the newly acquired revolvers were out of their holsters and aimed at the Texans. "Get back inside. I'll shoot the first man who goes for his gun."

Meekly they complied.

I followed at a discreet distance as Ben Thompson was escorted to the courthouse. I have never seen anyone look as amazed as Judge Osbourne was when my husband ushered in his prisoner.

"What's the charge?"

"It's pretty obvious, I'd have thought. Accessory to the murder of Sheriff Whitney."

The mayor looked serious. "Say, it's not that bad, young feller. Ben here was only acting up a bit, that's all. Make that a charge of 'disturbing the peace,' Judge."

Before anyone could say another word, the judge pronounced Thompson guilty. "Fined twenty-five dollars," he added.

Thompson paid his fine and left the courtroom, a free man.

I glanced at my husband's face.

He said nothing, just stroked his flowing moustache a little absently, but his eyes smoldered with resentment. Without speaking a word, he unpinned the marshal's star and placed it on the table in front of the judge. In a manner just as calm, he unbuckled the gun belt and laid guns and belt beside the badge. "I guess I won't be needin' these again."

"Hey, hold on a minute," the mayor said. "Yuh cain't leave Ellsworth like that, we need yuh. The job of marshal is yours—pays a hundred an' twenty-five dollars a month."

"Forget it, Mayor. What kind of town is this anyway? I risk my neck facing this man and his cronies, and bring him in without a shot bein' fired, or anyone getting' hurt, and what do you do? Charge him with breakin' the peace, fine him twenty-five dollars, an' turn him loose!"

The mayor looked embarrassed. "Yuh see, young man, we cain't afford to offend these Texas cowboys, they drive their cattle through this town every year and bring in a lot of business. But they need someone to keep them in order—and yuh're just the feller to do it."

"Sorry, gentlemen. I reckon Ellsworth is just too small an' mean for my tastes. Good day to you."

Turning, he held the door open for me to pass in front of him and walked out into the street. I linked my arm in his as we walked away from the courthouse.

"I'm real proud of you, dear," I told him, "though you really had me scared there, for a moment. But why didn't you take the job they offered? Everyone in Ellsworth respects you now, and the money's pretty fair."

He stopped for a moment, and it was a little while before he spoke. "Could you—" He laid special emphasis on the word. "—could *you* respect me if I was to throw myself in with the so-called law-enforcement officers in this town an' turn a blind eye whenever it was convenient to do so? It's a matter of principle, darlin'."

And that says it all. That's the way he is, and I have to admit that I wouldn't want him any other way. That's the man I married.

Maybe though, if he'd only sacrifice his principles just a little, he might be marshal of this town now, instead of his brother. Oh, but I shouldn't even be thinking such things, especially at a time like this, and I know in my heart I wouldn't really want him to change.

****

The Ellsworth incident happened seven—no, eight years ago. Time passes so quickly. My husband and his brothers were always close. When he decided to head for Arizona, his brothers came with him, and we all settled here. Our friend Doc Holliday, whose real name is John Henry, although no one ever calls him that, came too. It's been good here, until this stupid, wicked feud started up. The sheriff's as crooked as they come. He was put into office because of his political connections, and I reckon that was one of the things that brought about the feud.

The Clanton and McLaury gang rode into town this morning, seemingly thirsting for blood. As usual, the sheriff was nowhere to be found when he was needed. Virgil and the rest wasted no time in going after them.

I understand my husband well enough by now to know he'd always prefer to make an example of a man, rather than kill him, but maybe if he had shot Ike this morning, that would have been an end to the affair. Who knows? Instead, he disarmed the troublemaker and led him by the scruff of the neck to the courthouse where he was fined for a breach of the peace. He swore vengeance, and he and five of the gang made for the gun store. Then they sent a message, saying if the brothers didn't fight it out with them, they'd pick them off in the street—a challenge none of them could resist.

How long have I been standing here, staring through this window? A quick glance at the clock assures me that it has only been a few minutes. A few minutes? It seems like hours. Why haven't I heard any shots? What is happening? Anything would be better than waiting— waiting in the empty silence. Does he know how much I love him? Oh, if I never have the chance to say the words to him again…

I can stand it no longer. I shall go mad if I stay here any longer, wondering. I fling open the door and run down the stairs, almost tripping over my long skirts. Then I am running—running down the dusty main street of Tombstone toward the narrow lot at the rear of the OK Corral. I think I will never reach it, but at last I am there. I stop, trying to catch my breath. My blood seems to freeze in my veins as I survey the scene before me.

Sheriff Behan is making a half-hearted attempt to stop the trouble that is obviously about to erupt, but they push him aside and walk to face the McLaury and Clanton brothers.

I am unable to move from this spot. The sudden explosion of shots, when it comes, rips the silence asunder. I bite back a scream—I who have become so used to gunfire. The bay horse must have pulled itself free, for I hear the sound of hooves galloping up the street behind me. The poor thing must be terrified by all the shots. The exchange lasts for only a matter of thirty seconds or so, but it seems like an eternity to me. When it finally ceases, I release the breath I hadn't realised I was holding, and slowly open my eyes, dreading what I will see.

Three of the McLaury brothers and another man are lying dead in the blood and the dust. I turn my horrified gaze away from the blood-covered bodies, already swarming with flies, to where Virgil and Morgan lie, alive but wounded, how badly I cannot tell at this distance. Doc walks toward me, holding his arm, but the wound does not seem to be serious, thanks be to God.

I can hardly breathe for fear now, and my heart is thudding, my chest tightening. I peer through the gun smoke, which still hangs heavy in the air, stinging my eyes and making it difficult to see clearly, as I search in desperation for Wyatt, terrified by what I might find.

Then, two strong arms hold me close, and I thank the Lord he is safe—until the next time.

Six Hours or So

by

Lisa Wilkes

"You realize everyone thinks you're insane, right?" Josh asks as the 71 bus cruises to a stop in front of our feet.

Sunlight trickles down from above, warming my scalp. I crane my neck toward the sky, surprised by the brief respite from San Francisco's notorious fog. I'd checked the forecast three times today. There had been no mention of a fleeting appearance by the bright yellow orb.

Admiring the magnificent sky overhead, I utter a contented sigh. Then I shift my gaze forward and follow Josh up the stairs. "Is that so? Good crazy, or bad crazy?"

"Probably a neutral kind of crazy," Josh informs me. He taps his phone to the barcode scanner. I hold my breath while waiting to see if the finicky machine accepts our pre-paid tickets. To my delight, the box turns green, signaling our success in purchasing bus tickets online. "I mean, you're undeniably brave for moving from Richmond to San Francisco. But it's *bananas* to live 3,000 miles away from base. How long is your commute to work, five hours?"

"Six hours or so, with a headwind," I respond. "The good news is that I enjoy flying. It's in the job description."

Josh chuckles. The bus is packed to the brim, standing room only. We maneuver through a sea of strangers and wedge ourselves near the aft exit. Josh grabs a leather strap dangling from the ceiling. As the bus lurches forward, I wrap my arm around a metal pole.

"Luckily, you don't have to do that grueling commute very often, since you're a slacker," Josh teases as we cruise out of the Lower Haight. His lips contort into his signature smirk. "You hardly work, girlfriend."

"False," I insist, my voice rising an octave. "I do a ton of writing during the day, then bartend all night at the busiest restaurant in Potrero Hill. Sometimes I don't get home until sunrise."

"But you hardly ever *fly*, that's what I meant." Josh clears his throat. "Which makes commuting much easier."

"True. I couldn't keep up this charade if I had to fly a normal line. I'd be forced to move back to Richmond."

"Everyone at the base would be glad to see you."

"Don't they all think I'm crazy?" I chuckle.

"Yep. Doesn't mean they love you any less, though," Josh clarifies. "How long has your leave of absence been so far? Ten months?"

"Yes, ten glorious months in this glorious city." I gesture to the windows with my free hand. Lush palm trees and quirky storefronts provide an intriguing backdrop as we speed toward Union Square. "I fly one trip every two months, mostly to stay up-to-date at BrightCoast Airways. The rest of my time is spent here in the city of daydreamers and free spirits."

Josh smiles. "There's definitely a hippie vibe to this place. It suits you, Val."

"Thank you."

"Know what? Let the other flight attendants gossip about your insanity. I think you're a badass. You're not afraid to follow your weird little heart."

I snuggle into the crook of his arm, the way I would

lean against an older sibling for support.

"Thanks, Josh." My words are muffled by the collar of his shirt. "You always boost my self-esteem. No wonder you're my number one gay husband."

"Number one, huh? I'm honored."

I laugh. "You should be. There's a ton of competition at the airline."

The bus slows to a polite stop in front of Powell and Market. Doors fling open, beckoning us to explore the brightest, busiest part of the city. We dutifully obey.

Market Street is aglow with twinkling lights from dozens of boutiques. Josh and I stand still for a moment, side by side, and absorb the glittery scene before us.

A cool breeze blows past, whipping through our hair. Once the wind has subsided, I smooth down Josh's disheveled chestnut locks. Briefly, I envision us through someone else's eyes. We must be an interesting pair, two friends who know the loneliness—and the luxuries— of a vagabond lifestyle.

"Welcome to Union Square, the heartbeat of San Francisco." I lift an arm toward the skyscrapers surrounding us. "Sometimes I try to remember if I fell in love with SF right here. This might've been the spot. My memories are hazy, though."

"Why? Were you drunk?"

I shake my head vehemently. Brown hair cascades over my shoulder, several strands lodging themselves inside my coat. "Nope, I was delirious. Completely infatuated. San Francisco was everything I imagined it would be when my best friend and I used to talk about moving West."

"You've always wanted to move to California?"

"Hell yeah. Long before I became a flight attendant,

back when I was a college student in Ohio, I knew I had to see NorCal," I explain. "SF was this mysterious entity, this metropolis filled with culture and passion and art. It was everything my best friend, Breanna, and I wanted in life. Took me a long time to get here…but once I arrived, I knew I'd stay as long as possible. This place is breathtaking."

We stroll up Powell, past a series of retail stores and artisanal coffee shops. Josh walks beside me. His boots click sharply against the pavement.

"Is this still your favorite spot in the city, now that you've lived here a while?" he asks, somewhat breathless from the slight incline of Powell Street.

"Nah, not really. That title goes to Dolores Park or possibly the Lower Haight. It's hard to choose. Every section of SF has its own charm."

Josh exhales slowly, his breath an ephemeral white cloud. "Do you think it'll ever fade?"

"What? My love affair with San Francisco?"

He nods, green eyes brimming with curiosity.

"Doubt it. I love the Bay as much as I did when I moved here a year ago."

"Sounds like you're smitten." Traces of concern linger in Josh's voice.

I lift an eyebrow. "Is that a bad thing? I'm happy here; I get to chase after all my ridiculous dreams. In San Francisco, it's not weird to write songs and books and poetry. It's perfectly acceptable to have a service-industry gig and still pursue your own unique identity through whatever means you choose."

"Would you be okay if you had to leave?"

"Josh, are you trying to convince me to move back to Richmond?" I frown. "I love you, but I am not ready to say goodbye to this place. You should be glad I'm taking a leave of absence from BrightCoast. It boosts your seniority."

He wraps his arm around my shoulder. "Val, you've always been so cocky about that. It's two spots. *Two*. We are practically the same exact seniority."

"Except we aren't," I tease, a smile tugging at my lips. "I'm above you on every official airline list, pal. Sorry not sorry."

A few feet from us, a musician launches into a classic rock song. The guy can't be older than twenty. Fingers glide across guitar strings with grace and ease. The musical instrument seems to be an extension of his soul. He sways in rhythm with the song, closing his eyes as though nobody's watching.

"That guy isn't bad," Josh notes, jutting his chin at the shaggy-haired musician.

"All the street performers here are talented. They take pride in their music," I explain. "It means something to them."

"And you."

"Yes, and me."

Josh is quiet for a moment. "Seems like things fell into place for you so quickly, Val. One month, you and I are working the same line. I'm telling you about the handsome men I have crushes on. You're showing me the most beautiful parks and lakes in Minneapolis, Tahoe, Vermont. The next month, I see on Instagram that you've settled into an apartment in South San Francisco. Did you just resolve to move here, then go for it immediately?"

"Mmhmm. It took me a few weeks to get everything in order."

"But you followed through," he asserts. "Wow. You did it, Val."

"I did it," I echo. Linking my arm through his, I steer him toward an intersection lined with cable cars.

"Man, I wish I could stay longer," Josh murmurs. "Why can't layovers be a full week? It would be nice to spend more time with you. The Richmond base has been lonely without my favorite stewardess."

"That's sweet. Don't worry; you'll get another SF layover soon. We will still see each other," I predict. "In the meantime, I'd like to show you one more spot. When do you report for work?"

Josh glances at his wristwatch. "Shoot, I have to be back at the hotel within an hour."

"This place isn't far; we can make it. But we have to hurry." I grab his hand, lacing my gloved fingers through his. We zip down crowded streets. Our feet barely touch the sidewalk as we run toward my favorite bar in the city, an Irish pub that doubles as an open mic venue.

Inside, Josh orders a soda and I sip on a beer, a brown ale I've had once before. We spin our barstools to face the stage. A gorgeous woman sings into the microphone. Her lyrics drift through the dusty air and wrap themselves around us like candlelight, or the pulsing heat of a bonfire. This girl is compelling; she's got talent and charisma. She's eager to reveal her heart, one beautiful stanza at a time.

I smile at Josh, silently informing him this is the reason I'm enamored with San Francisco. He gives my hand a gentle squeeze. It's his way of telling me he understands.

During the train ride back to his hotel, he receives a text from the Lead flight attendant.

"My flight's delayed two hours," he says. "There was an unplanned aircraft swap."

I place a hand on his arm. "Dang. Sorry to hear that. If there's any silver lining, it gives us more time to hang out."

He grins in agreement.

We're both thoroughly exhausted after trekking all over the city. When the train pulls into the Millbrae station, we order an Uber to Josh's hotel, even though it's close enough to walk. Inside the car, I rest my head on Josh's shoulder. I wake up a few seconds later, no recollection of even closing my eyes.

"We're here, sleepyhead," Josh croons. He helps me out of the vehicle, joking that my ability to fall asleep anywhere is a sign of my old age.

Inside the hotel room, we curl up together on top of the bed, fully clothed. We have done this before, on various layovers in various cities. Josh makes me feel like a kid again, carefree and peaceful. Things are easy with him. He is the type of friend who consistently proves I'm not alone in this big, busy world.

Josh sets an alarm on his phone, then turns off all lights except one lamp in the corner. It emits a soft white glow, ideal for a quick nap.

I awaken to the shrill ringing of his alarm.

He sighs. "Forty minutes 'til my van to the airport."

"Did you get some rest?" I ask with a yawn.

"No, sadly. I couldn't sleep. There's something I really need to tell you. It's been weighing on me."

"What's wrong, Josh?" I ask, a lump forming in my throat.

"You're not going to like this. I'm so sorry."

I swallow, my voice lost someplace between my

chest and lips. I try to speak. It's an impossible task.

"I have been dating a crew scheduler for a couple of months," Josh says.

"Huh? That's great," I chime in. "I'm so happy for you, buddy. Is it anyone I know?"

"Maybe? I'm not sure. Federico, the nicest dude at headquarters. But that's not the point. He shared some news he wasn't supposed to, and I feel compelled to fill you in on this classified information. I don't want to alarm you, Valerie, but it affects you. Deeply."

I hoist myself up by my elbows, my stomach resting on top of the comforter. "You're scaring me, Josh."

"I don't want to see you get hurt."

"You can tell me anything. I'll be okay," I promise, even though I have no idea if that statement is true.

"BrightCoast is revoking every voluntary leave of absence," he blurts out. "They'll send a company-wide email within the next week. All flight attendants will be required to fly full-time again. I'm sorry, Val. I wish you could stay in San Francisco forever. You're thriving here."

I blink, unable to process my spiraling thoughts.

"Maybe you can live in SF and commute to Richmond. If anyone can make it work, you can," Josh tells me, his voice pleading. "It might not be so bad."

Tears form in the corners of my eyelids. "I haven't finished what I came here to do. I need more time."

"We are so young. We're not even thirty yet. You can accomplish anything you want, Valerie. There's no deadline."

"You don't understand."

"Help me, then. Tell me what you're worried about."

"My best friend and I always discussed coming to California." I lay down on my side and press my face to Josh's chest so I can avoid eye contact. "Breanna had a dream. We were both in love with the idea of chasing our art; she wrote songs, while I wrote short stories. She sang at every music venue in Ohio…and there weren't many, believe me. I published a few editorials in the college paper. Worked my ass off, but there was a limit to the success and exposure in a small setting like that."

"You wanted more," Josh ascertains.

"We wanted more," I explain into his chest. I sniff, silently begging my eyes to remain dry. "SF was the promised land. It was this place where we could be nerds and artists and dream-chasers and rule-breakers. It offered the exact thing we sought in life: freedom from the constraints of a rigid society. I'm not countercultural. I just wanted to be me. Breanna got it. She and I were cut from the same mold."

"You weren't just best friends, were you?" Josh asks softly.

I blink. Nobody's ever seen through the façade of plutonic friendship Breanna and I built over the years. "I loved her so much. I still do."

"Where is she now?"

"Right after graduation, she missed a stupid turn on a stupid street during a thunderstorm. She never made it home. Her car veered into a pole and she died instantly."

"I'm sorry."

"Me, too." Tears tumble down my face, despite my silent plea. Josh wraps his arms around me, his grip firm and reassuring. We lie on our sides, facing each other, my grief washing over him like a river of regret.

"Moving to SF was your way of honoring

Breanna?"

I gasp for air, struggling to regain composure. "Yes. I feel her all around me here. She never got to see this place, Josh. She was twenty-four when the accident happened. I applied to BrightCoast Airways a year later, maybe as a way to escape myself, I'm not really sure. Being a flight attendant meant I could travel the world and run from the things I wanted to forget."

"I think we all have that desire, deep down," Josh reflects.

"It worked for a while. Then I snagged a San Francisco layover and I knew I had to move here."

"Makes sense. SF is part of your love story."

"Absolutely. I can't leave just yet," I insist. "I haven't completed my goal."

"What's that?"

"To do things my way, however weird that might be. To share my writings with strangers. To laugh about the traditional life, made of picket fences and fake smiles and mundane jobs. I need to carve out my own corner of the universe, just like Breanna always wanted. Build a unique existence that feels honest and meaningful."

"I think you already achieved that," Josh surmises, adjusting his arms around my back. "You've never been plain or boring, Val. Come on, you are BrightCoast Airways' favorite wacko. People love your unapologetic quirkiness."

"Breanna wouldn't want me to give up so quickly."

"She'd be proud that you gave it your best shot," Josh corrects me. "You didn't just fantasize about heading West. You did it, girlfriend. Look where you are. You uprooted yourself and moved thousands of miles from base. Found a job bartending, set aside time every day to work on your writings. You made it happen. Breanna would celebrate this with you. I don't even know her but I'm sure she would raise a toast."

"Will everything change when I move back to Richmond in a few months?" I ask, prying myself from Josh's chest so I can wipe my eyes. "I love being a flight attendant. It's the only job that really matches my personality. I'll have no choice but to return to Virginia and live near the base. Do I lose myself to routine? Forget all about my goal of pursuing my craft?"

"Come on, we both know that won't happen," Josh tells me with a wink. "Look at you, Val. You're in touch with your emotions. You express yourself in vivid and relatable ways. If you move back to Richmond, you'll be the same amazing person you've always been. San Francisco didn't make you great, it just gave you a platform to grow and share your greatness."

"How can you be so sure?"

"Because I know you really well. Don't forget, I'm your number one gay husband," Josh declares proudly.

His cell phone rings, startling us both. Josh shows me the screen, illuminated with the words Screw Scheduling. I smile at the silly nickname for flight attendant schedulers.

"You think it's Federico?" I sit up and lean against the headboard. With the sleeves of my sweater, I dab at my eyes.

Josh shrugs as he answers the call. Even from several inches away, I can hear a shrill female voice on the other end of the line.

"Definitely not your boyfriend," I whisper. Josh utters "uh-huh" and "yep" and "thankya" as the woman at headquarters proceeds to fill him in on a change to his itinerary.

"Guess what?" he exclaims once the call is over.

"Umm, your flight's delayed another hour?"

He jumps to his feet. "Even better: the flight's been canceled. Our plane was taken out of service and it's too late to ferry in an aircraft from Seattle or San Diego. I get to stay here another night, my dear."

"Really? Josh, this is great. What do you want to do?"

"Call my crew and grab a drink at the hotel bar. Then we can go wherever you want. Let's make the most of the time. You should show off your fabulous terrain and enjoy every moment left in this city."

I nod. "Sounds good. Want to take a ferry to Sausalito? We could also borrow my buddy's car and drive to Napa. Or maybe ride the bus to Outer Sunset. Pass through Golden Gate Park, then grab dinner at a restaurant overlooking the beach."

"We can do whatever you'd like, Val," Josh says. "I trust your judgment."

"Good. I'm excited to show you more of this magical city."

He reaches inside the bathroom and picks up his toothbrush. Then he turns toward me. After a moment's deliberation, he speaks. "You're going to be fine, Val. I'm sure of it because I know the same secret Breanna knew, all those years ago."

I lift an eyebrow. "Oh? What's that?"

Josh smiles. "You contain the magic of San Francisco. It's inside you. It's always been there."

He disappears into the bathroom. I glance at the mirror on the wall, expecting to find smeared mascara and splotchy red cheeks. Instead, I am greeted by wide eyes. Despite the circumstances, they are clear and bright and hopeful.

I chuckle at the stubborn optimism embedded in my irises.

You'd love this place, I tell the soulmate I lost a long time ago. Thanks for bringing me here, on this wild adventure. Whatever happens next, I promise to make the most of it.

Prussic Acid

by

Melody DeBlois

In the summer of 1902, I first heard the dreadful news. A Miss Winifred Hutchinson, on holiday at Moffat, looked over the parapet of the bridge at Gardenholme Linn and saw, in the gully below, a human arm. Farther downstream, a pillowslip was retrieved. It contained a severed head, a thigh bone, a right forearm, and a blouse, the latter identified as one that had belonged to Olive Kent. Her mother recognized it by the patch under one arm. The pillowslip matched a sheet from Olive's bed and found under a microscope to be identical, both of the same loom, which in itself conveyed that in the end, Olive still had her pillow. (Although she had not slept in her bed for a long time.) Six months earlier, Olive Kent, my governess, disappeared from our house on Edinburgh Road.

Olive's mother, when I inquired at various times, sought to explain her daughter's absence by saying, "She went to Blackpool to nurse an ailing aunt." Then, "She's taken up with a sailor on the North Bank." Shortly after we received word of Olive's death, I questioned Mrs. Kent about the odd Frenchman to whom Olive appeared to be attracted—he had wooed her ardently, bombarded her with letters until she agreed to marry him.

Her mother broke down in tears and admitted he had been a frightful liar. He called himself Cab Horem, a man of violent nature who supposedly had been seen with a hotel chambermaid only hours before the poor dear turned up in a broom closet. Someone had suffocated her, apparently with a pillow. An ascot bound her ankles, and a handkerchief her hands. Safe to assume, the villain gagged her since no one in the hotel heard any screams.

Stunned, I holed up in my former governess's room. My dear, sweet Olive, with her youthful optimism, her contagious zest, had helped me cope after my mother died. Heart and soul, Olive gave me. I didn't mean to sound sentimental or overblown, but the truth was, I thought very highly of her.

It amazed me how few of her personal effects were missing. If she had run off with the Frenchman, it would stand to reason she would have taken more of her clothes, her diary, his letters still bound with ribbon. I found something rather curious in her nightstand.

It was an advertisement for a nursing home on Hertford Road in London. "Accouchement: Before and during, skilled nursing. Home comforts. Baby can remain."

Out of curiosity, I made the trip there, but I had no idea till I stood in the reception room in the establishment of how I would be received. I no more had a chance to examine the floor-to-ceiling bookshelves than a young, attractive woman entered. She was delicate and fine-boned, with the same ethereal eyes as St. Catherine of Siena. She introduced herself as Mrs. Amelia Sach and insisted I call her by her first name.

As if to confirm her goodwill, she had taken note of my interest in literature and set a volume of Wordsworth into my hands. She quoted in upper-class British:

"That blessed mood
In which the burden of the mystery
In which the heavy and the weary weight
Of all this unintelligible world

Is lightened."

I had not set out to deceive Amelia, but what better way to get to the truth than to feign a need of confinement I couldn't imagine. She listened to my narrative, her gaze resting pensively on my pocketbook with the rain glistening upon it. She tightened her shawl around her as I spoke, and often averted her glance to the dark passage beyond the open doorway. I had the distinct impression someone eavesdropped on my gloomy tale.

Amelia took my hand. "Rest assured, my dear, that for a tiny fee, your baby will receive a good home."

Father knew better than to dissuade me when I rang him. He knew me as headstrong as Mother had been, and this trait, he had confided, was one of her many endearing qualities. I could be histrionic and crafty when needed, and he understood the depth of my concern over our prior governess. In the end, he agreed to send me two hundred pounds on the condition that he alert the constabulary to the possibility of my being in danger.

I returned to the house in an hour. Dinner proceeded in the dining room, where dish covers rose into many feminine hands. Candlelight scattered light and shadow. The silhouettes sitting around the Dutch table rose against the wall like apparitions. The talk was commonplace, yet there seemed an aura of disturbing melancholy—a hush that spoke of innocence lost. I became more aware of their predicament when each misshapen figure rose rather awkwardly from her chair.

I counted fifteen who withdrew. I followed the women down a narrow hall. An oak door made a low moaning noise when I pushed it open. On the other side was a large and airy drawing room furnished with pieces from the Queen Anne period. Leather albums lay strewn about tabletops. Pictured in sepia-toned photographs were babies with their prestigious parents.

A woman, with an abundance of stomach beneath the gathers of emerald-green wool, passed me a stereoscope that held glass slides of Eleanor Roosevelt, the Astors, and a president or two.

"Our babies go to America where the rich and respectable adopt them in secret," she said. "But I've been informed mine is promised to a Vanderbilt."

"My dear friend recommended this establishment," I whispered. "You might remember her—Olive Kent?"

The woman patted the knot of golden braids in the back of her head. "Scarcely any of us go by our real names."

I gave her a brief description of my former employee, from which she became animated. "You mean, Hortense. I tried to talk her out of running off with the foreigner, but the last I saw her, she was slipping out amid a brutal storm. I never saw her again."

Amelia entered with tea, taking her seat in a stiff chair by the fireplace. We sipped the spicy, hot brew while she sang "Amazing Grace," and her eyes seemed to reach some infinite blue heights witnessed only by God's chosen few.

We went to our bedchambers soon after, and I found myself paired off with a woman whose features were sharp and dark. Her face was not beautiful, but a wistful depth occasionally played in her expression and brought to mind those moody portraits painted by Italian masters now long dead. Her name suited her, Isabella. She could be sullen and then riveted to attention all in the duration of a few lines of speech.

She tied her dressing gown above her voluminous stomach and then drew back the lace curtain. "He's out there, you know—the trespasser. Some claim he is waiting for Hortense, searching for her. I say he is hunting for another victim."

I tucked her into bed, and she elected to continue, "I'm going to him." She cradled her stomach with her long arms. "After I get rid of this. Do you find it quite incredible that I want to die?" She didn't wait for my response. "Some folks are touched by good. Not I. Ask my ma. She'll tell you soon enough."

There appeared nothing I could do to diminish her sense of guilt. Why was it a woman in Isabella's situation felt singularly at fault? How terribly unfair. My thoughts were cut short by a gradual sense I was being watched. With Isabella asleep, I tiptoed to the window.

There was no mistaking the man standing among the laurel. Olive had loved him. He had known the extent of her unshakable faith. I questioned the soundness of Cab Horem's mind as he remained in the moonlight like an angel who Lucifer had seen fit to empower. Something manic possessed him, and a savage look shown in his expression when he ventured closer.

The next morning, his grim image haunted me. Nearly oblivious, I didn't see the woman, a bucket of steaming water in her heavy arms.

"Get out of the way," she shouted.

"That's Miss Annie Walters, as coarse as dirt," Isabella informed me.

Miss Walters soon disappeared behind a door. Moaning drifted from the room, and then the sound of shuffling feet, of suppressed voices and sudden outbursts. After much time passed, I heard a long, quivering cry and a dull thud, a wail of loose springs as if someone had fallen against a mattress.

I started forward but was knocked aside by the mannish Miss Walters, a squalling baby in her arms. Two nurses accompanied her progress down the passage.

Inside the desolate room, I found the woman with her empress braids now unraveled down her shoulders. Blood stained the sheets as she lay there, solitary and abandoned. Tears trickled down her cheeks. I embraced her as she wept in anguish until, at last, she fell back and lost consciousness.

Night had set in when Cab Horem stormed through the front door. Amelia and Miss Walters were upon him and led him without hesitation into a back chamber. With my ear to the door, I heard him say, "I want my son."

"Why, so you can kill him like you did Hortense?" Miss Walters said acidly.

And Amelia spoke, "Because of our intervention, your child shall be saved from a life of poverty and wretchedness. You should get down on your knees, Mr. Horem, and give thanks."

"I must see the baby," he said. "I have—"

"Get out," Miss Walters cut him off, "or I fetch the constable."

Footsteps drew near, and I flew away from the door just before it opened.

I flinched at the sight of Cab Horem, pain-stricken and wild-looking, as he plunged down the corridor. I hadn't expected Miss Walters to turn in my direction. Her molten-gray eyes mocked me from her broad, homely face.

"You there," she spat through clenched teeth. "Are you spying on us?"

Before I could answer, Amelia came forward. "You poor girl," she said to me. "A man so far below your class. I shall ring Scotland Yard at once. We shouldn't have let this go on as long as it has."

Persistent questions plagued me: Why had the two women allowed their conflict with the man to go on at all? If they believed him guilty of such malice, why had they not notified the authorities when he first showed his face? If he had murdered Olive, why hang around to keep watch? To give concern over his presence when he was a prime suspect made no sense. Would he not run off in a panic if he was indeed the culprit?

I awoke in the night to Isabella's distressed cries and summoned help. Again, I leaned against a closed door, straining to hear. In the end, I crept into the room to see a strange bright light over a bed, Isabella, agony contorting her face, blackness all around, nurses who seemed to dissolve into the dark and to reappear in the concentrated whiteness. As long as I live, I shall never forget harsh Annie Walters slapping a naked baby, the infant's indignant cry, while Amelia Sach stood by like a sentinel, eyebrows quivering, mouthing prayers.

I should have given Isabella comfort in her despair. Instead, compulsive curiosity compelled me to follow Miss Walters out into the fog-shrouded morning. With a brown-paper parcel in tow, she boarded the underground.

Fifteen minutes later, she emerged from the train. I, having kept a safe distance, climbed the brick steps, then turned down a dark landing in time to see her discarding the parcel into a trash receptacle. She moved through the shadows, the pavement echoing footsteps that were solitary, no people around, for it was Sunday. The station proved dreary and cold. The horror of the silence grew within me. I could have sworn the pulsating of a heart came from the trash. At last, I opened the parcel, then closed it in revulsion.

The infant—Isabella's baby—shone a ghastly white, the pathetic, tiny body rock stiff, clad in a bloodied blanket. I didn't fathom until it was too late that the horrible Miss Walters, in stocking feet, had noiselessly crept back. Sneaking up on me, she had pulled a small revolver. She cocked the trigger. The sound reverberated throughout the empty corridor.

I cried out, "How pitifully easy it is for you to end a life that has barely begun!"

She pinned me against the brick wall. "A few drops of chlorodyne is all it takes." She held the gun to my head, a small vile in her other hand. "And now, dearie, how about a little drink of prussic acid?"

As I struggled to break free of the woman, I cried out. In the darkness, a face emerged, never a more welcomed sight, those huge, dark, savage eyes.

"Let her go," Cab Horem said just above our shoulders.

Miss Walters sprang away, rushing down the stairs, but Horem, perceiving her actions, fled over and blocked her escape. The gun fired, and in the next instant, Horem fell from the top of the stairs. His body thudded as the constable ran after the fleeing murderer.

In the darkness where I huddled frozen, I heard a crash. Knocked out and bleeding, Miss Walters lay insensible on the ground near to where Horem took a dying breath. I held him in my arms while Londoners gathered, and a police officer kept guard.

Cab Horem's last words poured out, "Olive, my goddess, my love."

Amelia Sach and Annie Walters stood trial at the Old Bailey before Mr. Justice Darling in January 1903. Being found guilty of numerous murders, they received a death sentence. They were the first women executed at Holloway Prison, following the closing of Newgate Gaol.

After saying good-bye to her own children, Amelia Sach, moments before her hanging, lifted her hands in prayer and said, "Sweet Jesus, know that I was being cruel to these unwanted babies only that I might be kind."